KID MOSES

KID MOSES

MARK R THORNTON

Arcade Publishing
New York

First North American edition 2015

Arcade Publishing books may be purchased in bulk at special discounts for sales promotion, corporate gifts, fund-raising, or educational purposes. Special editions can also be created to specifications. For details, contact the Special Sales Department, Arcade Publishing, 307 West 36th Street, 11th Floor, New York, NY 10018 or arcade@skyhorsepublishing.com.

Arcade Publishing® is a registered trademark of Skyhorse Publishing, Inc.®, a Delaware corporation.

Visit our website at www.arcadepub.com.

10 9 8 7 6 5 4 3 2 1

Library of Congress Cataloging-in-Publication Data

Thornton, Mark R.
Kid Moses : a novel / Mark R. Thornton. -- First North American edition.
pages ; cm
Summary: "The story of Moses, a nine-year-old survivor of the harsh streets of Dar es Salaam, Tanzania, who longs for something outside the grim existence he has known"-- Provided by publisher.
ISBN 978-1-62872-571-1 (hardcover : acid-free paper) -- ISBN 978-1-62872-633-6 (ebook) 1. Street children--Tanzania--Fiction. 2. Wilderness areas--Tanzania--Fiction. 3. Interpersonal relations--Fiction. I. Title.
PS3620.H78435K53 2015
813'.6--dc23
2015034229

Cover design by Shawn Paikin and Maggie Davey

Printed in the United States of America

For Toroye

Acknowledgements

Special thanks to Helen Moffett for her professional eye on numerous edits and to Daudi Peterson and Tessa Berlein for their reviews. I am also especially grateful to Neil Olsen, Jeannette Seaver, Maria Matthiessen, and Bridget Impey in South Africa who all made the publication of *Kid Moses* possible.

Part 1

Much later they sit under a tree, looking at the place where the snake has bitten Kioso. They have given up walking, not from being tired, or from the pain in Kioso's leg, or from any understanding of how snake venom works. They stopped because they were just not getting anywhere.

Moses sits doing nothing, not able to fix a venomous bite on a kid with no chance. They don't know much about snakes or any animals really, but they know enough to understand that they have reached a place they have never been before. The view before them seems different. They are not philosophical enough to wonder if this valley will be the last thing Kioso will see, or if the ground under this tree will be the last place he will visit, or if there will be any final moment of transition or clarity. They do not seek frantically for a solution, a way out, a cure, or a poultice to prolong Kioso's life. They cannot run, and there is no place they can go that seems better than where they now sit.

Kioso's leg swells fast, reminding Moses of the bloated, dead-men legs of the homeless people back on the streets of Dar es Salaam. The leg bulges and takes on odd shapes. The skin is tight and hard and its surface smooth, like the stomach bladder of a slaughtered goat.

The leg keeps changing. Moses looks away at the valley, then at the land behind, then at Kioso's face. And when he looks back at the leg, a new bulge has appeared under the skin, or a new kind of seeping stuff is dripping down the leg like cooked fish fat. The leg takes on not just a shape, but a life and evolution of its own. Both boys just sit back and watch it. Almost as if putting some distance between them and the leg will prevent it from jumping altogether on top of them.

The venom finally reaches Kioso's brain. The formula of toxins designed for the simple destruction of a field-mouse has crept northwards, from leg to knee, up thigh and through the vast interior of his body to arrive in his head and the sensations of his mind. Kioso mumbles, sweats, panics, grabs Moses's arm, and then falls into a dreary sort of sleep that is not real sleep, but respite for a period of time from reality.

Death crawls into his bones. Or rather, gnaws its way there. Kioso does not know he is dying. He just knows he is scared, and doesn't have the strength to do anything. He looks up at Moses with eyes like those of a begging dog. Some drool slides from his mouth. He is thirsty, then has brief jolts of pain. Death takes him as he gazes skyward into the thin canopy of acacia trees.

Moses buries him under a tree. He uses a stick and his hands, and he digs for a long time, but the ground is too hard, so he rolls Kioso into the shallow scrape and then puts the earth back over him. When he first throws the earth onto him, it goes onto Kioso's face and into his mouth, and Moses stops. He wants it to be over him all at once. He hates seeing bits of Kioso's body exposed—his shoulder sticking up—because he can't dig a deep-enough hole. He panics and squeezes his eyes shut and sits on the ground to shovel in the earth with his feet so he does not have to stand there and throw it onto him.

And then Moses walks—it is what he knows how to do, if nothing else. Thirst and hunger are now permanent aspects of life. He finds a rocky outcrop just high enough to give him a view, and climbs up. From the top he can see out across the vast expanse of trees. There is nothing so flat in the world as the giant land before him. Not even the ocean back in Dar es Salaam seemed this flat. But now that he has found the view, he doesn't know what to do with it. It means nothing to him. He cannot figure his direction. Instead, he turns to where the land looks slightly less hostile, and goes there.

After some days, the trees begin to thin out and the country opens up into plains and scattered woodland. Spindly trees come up from the earth like old women's fingers. He finds water in a couple of small mud holes. But food, no. He tries to eat some leaves, but they make him vomit, and he does not try them or any other leaves again. He finds a honeybee hive, and sits at a distance watching the bees, not wanting to get stung.

It all seems distant to him now. Not just Kioso's death, but the school, the harbour, living on the streets back in Dar es Salaam. He sings Radi Bundala in his head. At times his mind is blank, numb, and then the songs just appear there. He will be walking along, or sitting in the shade and then: "Listen to me child. There is nothing for you in this town . . ."

Again and again the songs play in his mind, like he is walking with some sort of companion. It makes him think of the harbour, of the old days. Despite the struggles of his life there, the thought of it is familiar, and he takes comfort from thinking about their names—his and Kioso's—etched in the wood at their old sleeping spot in the rotting ship hull.

Moses keeps walking. He stops to rest sometimes, but soon feels that he too will die if he just sits, and this pushes him on, slowly but to somewhere.

Eventually, he does not think of Radi's songs, and his fatigue reaches the point where no music plays in his mind.

Chapter 1

Moses came out of his sleeping place and into the dusty seaside world of Dar es Salaam. He made for the main road—always good at that time of day, with all the people going to work and moving about. He crossed the rail-line and the small field after it, and continued along the dirt streets to where the big avenue stretched out wide, with palm trees and shops and banks and people crowded along its sides. It was already hot, and the big road was loud. Fare-collectors shouted from the *matatus* with all those people inside going somewhere.

Moses stood in the street and pointed his fingers together at the thumb, motioning towards his mouth: "Give me money." Windows rolled up and he pressed his face against them. Drivers looked at him and said no, or looked ahead and pretended he wasn't there. Walking people moved around him so not as to brush against his dirty body or be touched by his grubby hands.

"Don't beg," some said. "Don't touch me. Go away."

Then a woman approached: "Come with me." She took Moses's hand in hers, and they walked. The woman was big and walked slowly, her ankles thick and spilling out over her shoes. They came to a corner where a man sat on a crate roasting maize over a small fire. The woman handed the man a coin, then took an ear of maize for herself, and handed one to the child. "You say you are hungry, then eat."

Look at this filthy child, she thought. That brown shirt with no sleeves was probably white at one time. Hands black with dirt, teeth yellow and brown, bits of dried grass stuck in his hair. How old, even? Nine? Ten, maybe? And he holds the maize with such dirty hands, rubbing them all over his food.

"Well, say thank you, at least," she said as she wiped her hands with a handkerchief. "And you go safely, you." So he did, and she left him and walked on, and he returned to the big avenue.

At dusk he left the streets, careful to avoid the bored and lonely men who guarded the shops at night. Some of his friends had been taken by them before, into hidden places in the alleys. But he knew that nobody could find him in the old ship hull at the harbour. It was where he and some of the other kids from the street had made a home of sorts, a haven. So he headed there.

It was cramped, but safe. He crawled down inside the hull and squeezed through some loose planks to a place in between the boards just big enough for a handful of small children to sleep. Soon his friend Kioso arrived. He had managed to get some bread and bananas. Moses shuffled over to make room for him to sit down. They made a small fire from scraps of cardboard, and Kioso laid the food out and they began to eat.

Above them were the sounds of the night, the men from the street, coming to their place in the rotten ships along the harbour's edge. Their shouts were always loud, cries of frustration and madness. The men would be drunk and the women expressionless, going to and returning from the corners of the harbour with their customers. And then the fights and smashed bottles and the crashing of men jumping from chairs and stools. One yelling about a knife, a cry, and then the clattering of boots as the men ran down the harbour road.

The morning looked and felt different. Rays of sunlight found their way into the hull of the old ship. The beams of yellow crisscrossed Moses's face as he sat up to look out over the blue water. The harbour was quiet. The men above were rising slowly to cigarettes, or not yet rising at all. He had sneaked up on them before as they lay passed out, dipping into their gloomy places, over the broken glass, between the crates and fallen chairs. Slipping gently into their pockets, crawling around them silently, combing them for money, cigarettes, watches. But that was dangerous work, and he and Kioso still had food. So they finished the rest of the bread.

The only other sounds were from the old men, the ones who had survived the harbour the longest, the ones who sifted through the morning rubbish before people woke up. Fantastical creatures, missing eyes, fingers maybe, and clothed in tangles of shirts and rags and plastic bags. Like angels or phantoms or beasts from some unknown place, shuffling along the harbour road.

Moses stared into the sun, thinking of the uncle who was supposed to take him to school and give him clothes and food. But just never did. Just beat him until Moses left, one day gone, and that was it. And before that, his father who went to load crates at the harbour every morning for a daily wage. Working for meagre pay that couldn't feed the family, only enough for a cup of watery *uji* in the morning. And his mother who ran away somewhere after his father was killed.

But his father had spoken of good things. He was from a farm, and had come to the big city for the good life, like so many others. From a place up in the mountains where people grew bananas and vegetables and maize and even coffee, to a place of struggle and waiting for things that never came.

"We will go to the farms one day, Moses," he would say.

Moses remembered them talking outside their shack, his father's hands brushing the dust from his pants and shirt. With big eyebrows, he had smiled down at the boy: "When I get enough money from the docks, we'll go back and build a house to live in, and have money to buy things from the shops. And even a bicycle for you, maybe."

Moses loved the idea of riding a bicycle past farms, down a road to a shop with big barrels of sugar and meal and rice inside in the shade, and all those items hanging on strings from every corner, no inch of space wasted. He imagined how he would lean his bicycle against the wall of the shop, keeping an eye on it so nobody would steal it, and how he would go inside and buy a soda, and then sit outside by his bicycle drinking it, and watching the people looking at him.

❁

The next morning, as it turned out, was the day Moses would remember as the one when it all began. He and Kioso had not planned to go anywhere, but a lorry had passed and they had hopped aboard. One minute they were playing in the street, asking for change, stealing oranges from the street vendor with clubfeet, and the next they were hiding under a canvas tarpaulin in the open cargo bed of a lorry leaving town.

Moses had been thinking of his father more often than usual, and of farms, any farm, just the idea of a farm. Over the days, the thoughts had turned into possibilities, the idea of a farm becoming a chance to take. The boys had no plan or idea of which direction to take, how to go, or what to do when they arrived there, wherever "there" turned out to be. They simply hopped on and went.

The lorry was blue and left a cloud of lead-smoke behind it as it bounced on leaf springs too tight for an empty load or for travel on a corrugated road of holes. Moses and Kioso peeked out from under the canvas cover sometimes, but mostly they lay low and bounced about the big, empty, open bed of the lorry. At first it was exciting, then funny, then boring, and then scary.

After a couple hours, the lorry stopped. Men got out. The boys stayed quiet and kept the canvas tarp over their heads. The men opened the bonnet of the lorry and poured water into the hissing radiator. Then they climbed back in and drove on. They passed through a town, then another, where they stopped to buy cigarettes, and carried on again. When the lorry slowed for a big bump or a deep hole, the dust would overtake it and envelop the lorry and fall onto the tarp in the back. Fine particles would form clouds so thick that their glimpses of the sky were blocked out.

They passed through more towns and then small villages, climbed some hills, crossed a river, and the land stayed bumpy, the boys bouncing about the lorry bed along with the leftover fruit. Villages then became scarce, and the boys sat low, exhausted and abused by the banging of the lorry on the road.

They listened to the gears of the lorry, to the strain of the old engine. They peered out to watch the tops of the trees passing by and the sky and the clouds overhead changing from everywhere in the morning to bubbly at midday to flat like the tops of the trees in afternoon, and then to nothing at all. Sometimes they could see signboards along the road, but after a while these too became scarce. They passed fewer trucks and cars, until eventually the road was empty except for them.

Moses thought of their options. Jump out now or stay longer? They were scared of being discovered and scared of the men. Boys like Moses and Kioso didn't like men or trust them either. To boys like Moses and Kioso, men only meant getting yelled at and kicked and beaten.

There were a few decent men at the harbour, mainly the old ones, who were just too old to be trouble. The phantoms who just minded their own business and hobbled along the streets, waiting for their day to die. The orange vendor with the clubfeet wasn't a bad man either. He yelled at the boys and shook his stick at them, but nothing more than that.

It was the younger men who were the problem. They thought they were big men, especially when they were with girls and other young men. They didn't have anything though, no jobs, nothing. Just size. They would beat the boys sometimes, and take whatever they had and throw it on the ground and laugh. Sometimes they had knives to show to each other and whistle at.

And of course there was Prosper. He looked young, but he always had people around him, willing to listen to him and be a part of his gang. Maybe it was because he never smiled. Maybe because he did everything first. Maybe because he wasn't afraid to talk big.

Either way, Prosper hung around the market like the others, waiting for night-time to do his stealing. He didn't necessarily dislike the young streetkids, but he hassled them and beat them as part of his routine. And he didn't necessarily dislike Moses more than any other kid, but Moses always seemed to be crossing paths with Prosper—and was always trying to get out of his way.

Moses thought of Prosper and thought of the men driving and knew that eventually they would stop at their destination and pull back the tarpaulin and find the boys.

So they jumped. One and then the other, they fell and bounced in the dirt and scurried with bloodied knees into the bush. The truck bounced along at the same speed and with the same noise, coughing its way down the road until it was gone and its banging heard only occasionally, and then not at all.

Moses and Kioso watched the dust settle. Quiet returned to the scene. A dove flew onto the road and pecked at its stones. The world around them became a world of wilderness, with just a small road passing through it. Moses lifted Kioso up by the arm. He wiped blood from his knees and elbows and brushed the sandy stones from the scrapes. He looked down at the road and then into the woodland around them.

"Where are we?" Kioso asked.

Moses walked down the road a little way and then back, and then in the other direction, and back again. Kioso looked at Moses, waiting for some solution. Moses brushed his head with his hand. "I don't know where to go or which way is better."

The two stick-figure children remained standing in the road, afraid to move as the sun got lower and the birds started moving to their places in the treetops where they would spend another night safe, nestled together, wings in tight, heads tucked down in their feathers.

The land cooled and the flies stopped buzzing. Like the harbour at night, where people changed from beggars into drunks, from sleeping people in the afternoon into violent men at night, here too was a transition at dusk.

But for Moses and Kioso, the routines of this night were new. New sounds emerged from the bush as darkness came. Vision was no longer the primary sense. Instead, the ears awakened. Scratching noises could be heard from within trees, walking-animal noises from the bushes, and the strange sounds of flying things whisked above them and sometimes close to them, almost brushing their faces. The night got cold too, not like at the harbour. The earth lost its heat, and the boys curled in the ditch by the road.

We shouldn't have jumped, Moses thought. Those men beating us would have been better than this. Animals all around. I can hear them. All these noises, and it's cold, and there are things crawling in the leaves in this ditch.

Just keep still and don't move, he thought. Don't make a sound. I think Kioso's sleeping. I am too tired to look after him right now. It's cold up here and there's nothing we can use to get warm. Just sitting here, holding my knees. There must be more cars on the road. We shouldn't have jumped.

"What's that noise?"

"Nothing, Kioso. Just go back to sleep."

"How are we going to get back to Dar?"

"Don't know yet."

"I want to go back."

The harbour. I could be sleeping in the ship now. Fast asleep, not cold. Could have maybe gotten leftover food from the restaurant. And today's Friday. Could have gotten some money from the shops. Those Muslims always give money on Fridays.

Mika and Heriel are probably at the ship now, sleeping like I could be. Maybe Ali has come back, too. Don't know where that kid went. He's been gone a while. Who knows where anyone goes?

✹

Kioso slept that night, but Moses never did. He sat, eyes open in the darkness until the moon rose, casting light over the world. It was a big moon and the light mostly shone onto the road, but some filtered through the tree canopy and Moses looked up at the shapes above him. It was colder than any night he had ever experienced, and he sheltered Kioso, giving him warmth from his body.

Moses watched the night mature and the moon travel overhead. Then he watched dawn come with cold, blue light and low fog over the earth. The sun rose higher and finally he felt its warmth on his feet. He was determined not to spend another night sleeping in a ditch.

"Kioso, get up. We're leaving."

"I'm hungry. You hungry?"

Moses looked at Kioso and did not answer.

"We're leaving here now."

Hungry, he thought. Yes, I'm hungry. Of course I'm hungry. Standing in this road again, looking down that way, just dust and trees. And this way, just the same. Moses knew that before they had jumped out of the lorry, they hadn't passed any villages for a long time, and they hadn't seen any signboards either. Just trees. To head back the way they had come would be a long and lonely walk. So Moses decided that going forward was the best option. Into the unknown, but with a chance at least.

"We're going this way. There must be a village or people or something. Maybe a car will pass by anyways."

"But Dar is back that way, the way we came."

"Yea, but there was nothing for a long time. Remember? And if a car passes us going that way, we can get a lift maybe. But for now, let's walk on. Maybe we will get to something."

Kioso whined for more answers when there simply weren't any. Moses almost snapped at him, but didn't.

"C'mon, Kioso. Just follow me."

Moses began to walk down the road, the dust not yet flying, the land still cool and calm. Kioso climbed out from the ditch and trotted along behind him, anxious to catch up. And the two boys, in red sandals and dirty shirts, were small on the wide road as they walked on.

At first, they looked around as they went, at the trees, into the woodland around them, in the ditches, for something, anything. The trees were thick with big leaves, but not lush like back in Dar. It was dry. At first, when a noise came from somewhere off the road, they would stop and hold still and strain their ears to hear it again. But after a while, they just kept on walking. The narrow road was crowded in by tall trees, and when Moses looked into the surrounding wilderness, he saw a mass of endless woodland, thick, looking all the same. It seemed that if they were to walk off the road, even a few steps, it would be hard to find it again. The bush would swallow it. The road, so certain when one was on it, would simply fade into the expanse of vegetation and grass.

They carried on for a long time with no cars coming, and the day began to get hot. They rested in the shade for some time. And then they continued walking.

"Wo! What's that?"

"What?"

"That's a snake!"

"That's a stick."

"No, that's a snake."

"I never seen a snake that big before."

"I did one time. Dead on the road. A green one, really long. Don't touch it."

"Is it dead?"

"Don't get near it."

"It's big."

"Maybe it's sleeping. It'll bite you, you know. And you'll die, because they have bad poison."

Kioso approached warily, ready to jump back. Moses found a stick to poke the snake.

"You crazy. That thing will kill you."

"Na, it's dead. Look at its head, all smashed in. Got run over."

Moses tried to lift the snake with the stick, but it broke. He found a bigger stick, but he still had to use both hands to lever up the snake. "Here, look at it," he said, shoving the snake towards Kioso.

"Don't throw that thing over here!"

Moses stopped and looked up the road. "Shh, what's that noise?"

He stood still, the dead snake now at his feet, with Kioso also listening.

"What do you h—"

"Shh!"

Sometimes the noise would die out, but then come back. A low drone, then the occasional bump.

"A car. Coming from up there. Going back that way. To Dar. We got to try to get on."

An old grey Peugeot drove slowly towards them and stopped, its engine still running. A white man sat inside. The car's small engine idled in a weak purr, as the man leaned out the window. His movements were slow, strange, and the boys edged back from him.

The man was old and grey-haired. He wore a stained, short-brimmed hat. Moses looked at his face. His nose was huge and full of holes and pointed like a woman's shoe, and his face was spotty like all other old white men, but more so.

At first, he looked at the boys, his eyes bright blue, almost white, and then he opened the car door to step out. Moses and Kioso backed away. But the man squatted down and told them in Swahili that it was all right, there was no need to run.

"Where can you run off to anyways?" he said, smiling. "There is only bush here. And you don't want to go in there, because it's dangerous."

He motioned to the trees with his arms, still squatting, and then opened them towards the boys. "Come. It's okay."

He moved slowly like any other old man, Moses noticed, but he kept twitching his fingers. And his car was old. What was a white man doing with such an old car?

"Kioso, come over here." Moses grabbed his arm and pulled him closer.

The man rose and stood over them.

"Where are you two boys going?"

Moses looked up the road.

"Trying to get back to Dar. But walking that way."

"Dar?" The man cocked an eyebrow, and then squatted again.

"I am going that direction. Not all the way to Dar. But you can come with me and get part of the way back. Get in. You can have a nice meal." He smiled, showing big yellow teeth, and opened his arms again, as if a man waiting to be hugged by his grandchildren.

Moses looked up the road and then at Kioso, who just stared back at him. All the nerves in his body told him to get away from the man, to keep walking. The instincts that had kept him alive on the streets of Dar told him so.

But the boys got in, Moses in front, Kioso in the back seat, and the man drove slowly down the dirt road. Moses sat close to the door, far from the man. Whenever he looked over at him, their eyes would meet, and Moses's heart would jump, and he would look back at the road.

"Where are we going?" he asked.

The man smiled back at him. "Oh, not far."

They passed the spot where they had jumped off the lorry, and then a few farms. Moses was relieved at the thought of finally being out of the empty wilderness. The man's house was off the main road and up a rough narrow track leading into the hills. When they arrived, the house stood decayed and small in a yard of weeds with trees all around. A car with no doors lay rusting in the yard. The man pulled up next to it and stopped. "Here we are. Go inside, boys."

The man had no help, no maid or garden boy, which was strange, Moses thought, especially for a white man. But he heated a meal of leftover beans, and the boys sat inside on the floor on a worn, yellowed sheepskin. The man didn't speak any more, but kept glancing back and forth between the stove and where the boys sat. Eventually he placed a tin bowl of food down in front of them. He told them to eat and sleep if they wanted, and went outside onto the steps and sat down. Moses had forgotten how hungry and tired he was, and the boys ate quickly. After they finished, Kioso was asleep on the sheepskin within a few minutes. Moses didn't intend to sleep, but he also did. The house was so quiet.

When Moses woke up, it was getting dark, and things were different inside the house. The man sat at the table with a bottle of liquor and a glass in front of him. He was watching the boys.

Moses looked at the man staring at them. His mouth was wet and pink and his hair was matted down where his hat had been. There were no lights in the house, just the blue-grey colour of the last breath of day creeping in through the windows. The house was still, no wind finding its way inside or through the trees in the surrounding forest.

Moses watched the man pour more brown liquor into his glass and drink. He set the glass down gently, but unsteadily, and then rose and took three uneven steps to the counter by the sink, and switched on the radio.

The tinny sound of Soukous music rattled from the small radio and the man drank again from the glass. Moses nudged Kioso, who woke up, turned over and looked at the man.

"What YOU looking at?" said the man, with spit bubbling on his bottom lip.

Kioso sat up on the sheepskin and looked away. Moses glanced at the door, at the window, the radio, the bed by the wall. His heart was beating hard now. He thought in rapid succession of the way they had come up to the house—the main road, the dirt track, the rusted car in the yard—and then the way he had felt when the man had first approached them on the road.

"Little monkeys. Lost on the road, you were. With nowhere to go."

He sang slowly at the ceiling. "Nowhere to go . . . Nowhere to go."

"NO—WHERE—TO—GO," he repeated, louder, sliding his head back and forth with each word.

Then he rose and came closer, hovering over them, a giant creature filling the room. He squatted, his face close to Moses's. Moses could smell beans and liquor. The man's eyes were watering, his lips sucked together. He looked sick, his patchy skin like porridge, pale and cratered. Moses turned away and hunkered closer to Kioso, the two now linking arms.

The man grunted and rose with effort, returning to the table. He started to sit, but then he turned, walked to the door and went outside. Moses could hear his boots clunk on the steps down into the yard. He heard the zipper of the man's pants, and then him pissing in the dirt. A long, wobbly-legged drunkard's piss.

"Moses." Kioso sat upright and looked at Moses with fear.

"I know. We're going to leave."

Moses thought of the possibilities, various images racing around his head. Moses remembered the men on the streets who took small boys. Kioso had been caught once.

He's still pissing, Moses thought. Still outside. What's he doing here living in this house? Why did we get in that car? He's drunk, and what is he going to do all night? We can't sleep here. Maybe he'll pass out. Maybe we should just wait for him to drink more and go sleep on that bed. Then we can leave or maybe wait until morning. And outside? Don't know where to go there. Except for that track leading down to the road.

The man stopped pissing and Moses listened to him climb the steps to the door. But then he stopped. Moses watched the door, the doorknob, the crack beneath the door. He squeezed Kioso's hand, thinking of how to run, when to make a dash. He waited for the man to enter, but the man just stood outside. Moses could see the shadows from his boots under the door. Just standing there, not moving. For some time there was no sound.

Then the doorknob turned and the shadow of the man came inside. For a moment, he lingered tall in the doorway, his hand still on the doorknob as if to hold himself up. And when he staggered back to the table, they ran.

The two little monkeys jumped at the door, feet quick like they were back at the harbour, the market, the street.

But the man lunged across the small room and snatched Kioso by the arm.

"NO. You are NOT leaving." His jaw was flexed and his lips hidden inside his face, bent with anger.

"Let him go! Kioso—come on!" Moses grabbed Kioso's arm. The man pulled Kioso one way and Moses tugged him the other, towards the open door. Kioso's little body was spread, almost comically for a brief moment, before he cried out and the man punched him. His solid fist slammed down into Kioso's head, and he crumpled like a cut weed. Moses crouched in the doorway, facing the man, who still held the arm of Kioso's limp body, like a shot rabbit carried by the ears.

Only a second passed before Moses ran. He leapt down the steps and bolted for the trees. He heard the man stumble after him, and then fall hard and loud down the steps, crying out. Moses could not hear his words, only the hugeness of his voice. He ran through the forest and through the darkness. One of his sandals was gone, but he kept going, feeling the branches cutting his legs and the stumps and roots hammering his feet. Moses knew how to run. He knew that with men, you run and never stop. If you stop, you get beaten. If you stop, you get your pants ripped and get fucked.

He fell, got up, and kept running. He fell again and cut his knee. As he went through the trees, he thought of Kioso with the man. He had hit him hard, Moses thought. Kioso—I hope you can get out. But you were down like a dead kid. No way you can run. That man's got you, Kioso, and I can't go back. He'll get me too, so I can't help you.

Eventually the trees started thinning, and the land became open fields of dried maize stalks, some as tall as Moses. He slowed to a fast walk. He passed through the maize stalks in the dark, feeling his way forward, parting the tall crops with his hands as he went. Through a field and then another, under a fence, and onto a dirt road. He walked down along it, but carefully and by the side of the road. He knew that if something came past, he could jump into the bushes alongside. But it was dark and quiet. He could not see well, but he knew that he was bleeding from the cuts on his feet and knee.

Night-time again. He paused and looked back and then up at the sky for some reason he did not know. It was suddenly very dark, with clouds rolling above. No moon, no stars, just blackness. He felt his way off the road and into the tangle of undergrowth, touching the air in front of him, searching for a place that felt safe enough to lie down. His mind was full of images of snakes, like the one they found on the road. The thought of stepping on a snake terrified him, as he poked his way through the leaf litter, twigs snapping under his feet. He found a ditch and crept into it. Just like last night, just like a goat. Some animal sleeping outside in the bushes, in the fields.

Moses curled in the cold and thought about Kioso. Would the man kill him? Maybe he would just beat him and throw him out the house. Maybe Kioso would also escape and come down the road and find him. Kioso was smart. He knew how to get by. Moses tried to think of good ways for the story to end, imagining Kioso escaping, even killing the old man, and running through the forest like Moses had done.

And then thoughts of the bad things came, images in his mind of the dark house and the liquor. Of men and violence, those common features in his life. His thoughts jumped back and forth between the bad things, the good things, and then finally they settled on how he had abandoned Kioso. He pulled his arms in closer to his body and acknowledged: "I left him behind."

The next morning came early for Moses. He woke just as it was getting light and set off walking again. His feet were sore and cut, especially the one that had lost a sandal. The road was quiet and nothing seemed to be alive. No birds sang. There was a low damp mist around the trees and fields. As he walked, he started to think about the day before, and about Kioso still back with that man.

After some time, he heard a car and hid himself in the trees to watch it come down the road, in case it was the white man in his grey Peugeot. A different car appeared, also old, but packed with a family and driving slowly, scraping its undercarriage on the road. A man and his wife sat in the front, and the arms and peering faces of their kids poked out the back windows. As the car drove down towards him, Moses stepped into the road to wave it down.

The woman in the front seat saw Moses and elbowed her husband. "Who's that boy in the road?"

The husband shrugged.

"What's he doing in the road like that? I've never seen him before. Not any of the kids from that farm there."

The husband looked at her, shrugged again, and looked back at the road. The woman turned her eyebrows in and looked more closely. Something was wrong, she knew—the way the boy stood, the way he held himself by the edge of the road at that hour of the morning.

"Stop up there next to him. Just pull up alongside him. Here. Here. *Simama hapa.* Stop here."

They pulled up next to Moses.

"Hey, child, what are you doing here? Where are you going? Where are you coming from? What happened to your feet?"

"I need a lift."

"Where? Yes, well, get in, child. We'll take you. What's wrong with your feet? Where are you coming from?"

Moses approached the car with caution. The woman opened her door and Moses squeezed in next to her. Her children watched silently from the back, and the man just watched it all from the side.

"Don't you be scared, child. I'm Mama Tesha."

The woman looked more closely at Moses, at his feet, his shirt.

"What happened? Tell me, where you need to go?"

Moses did not answer the woman, just looked at her. She was massive and her bottom filled most of the front seat, her husband just a thin stick beside her. Her eyebrows were stern, but her skin and lips looked soft. She held a black handbag on her lap and was wearing a nice dress, which squeezed in her wide bottom and breasts.

They reached the main road and drove until they reached a town. They stopped by a small shop and the husband turned off the engine. The children jumped out of the car and the husband opened his door and stepped out. Mama Tesha stayed in the car with Moses.

"So tell me, child. I don't know where you want to go to."

She looked down at Moses, who stayed silent.

"Okay, where do you live?"

"Dar."

"Dar es Salaam?"

"Yes."

"Dar! What are you doing way out here? How did you get here?" Moses told the woman about the lorry, the old grey Peugeot, the man, the house and the liquor and Kioso. He told her about running through the forest and then sleeping by the road. Mama Tesha thought for a while, and clicked her tongue. Then she took Moses by the hand and walked down the dirt road to the town's small police station.

The police building was low and had an iron-sheet roof. It had once been whitewashed, but was now stained with birdshit and age. On the walls inside, there was a framed photograph of the president and a few yellowed papers tacked to a board. A policeman sat at a chipped wooden desk with a couple of drawers left open. On the desk was a rubber stamp, an inkpad and some loose papers, and behind him more papers were stacked and covered in gecko droppings. Mama Tesha and Moses approached.

At first, Moses was silent—he didn't like police. To him, they were just like the young men at the market and no better. But Mama Tesha made him feel safe, and after some time he spoke, telling the man in his white police uniform the same story he had told her, where the house was, and what had happened there. The policeman sucked food from his teeth and wrote notes slowly. Other policemen came out of other rooms, and they all chatted back and forth.

The men took Mama Tesha aside and talked to her for a short while. Then they leaned down and told Moses that they knew the man he was talking about, and where he lived. They told him that he should wait at the police station with the woman, and that they would go to the man's house to find Kioso.

Much later, they came back. The police had found the man's house, but no car and no man and no boy. Once again they spoke to Mama Tesha. Then they all stood in front of Moses and explained to him that Mama Tesha had been visiting family on the nearby farms, but was now travelling back to Dar where she lived. They said that he should drive back there with her, and that he would be safe. They told him that when they found Kioso, they would call her. One policeman leaned forward and held a piece of paper out in front of him for Moses to see.

"See? We wrote this mama's telephone number on this slip of paper." He nodded in Mama Tesha's direction. He pointed at the paper and looked at Moses. "We will keep this number, and when we find your friend, we will telephone her, and she will tell you. Don't worry. We will find your friend."

Moses climbed in the car with the woman and her family, and they drove off back down the road to Dar es

Salaam. And as they left the station, the policemen rose to go and drink tea, and the slip of paper slid to the floor and under the desk and to a place where things remain for a long time.

Chapter 2

Moses stayed that night in Dar in the home of Mama Tesha and her family. He didn't sleep. He just lay there, listening to the sounds of the sleeping: the woman snoring and her husband and the many children breathing throughout the small house.

He had seen kids disappear, even get killed a few times. He had seen other people die, had seen a car accident with a man and three women pulled out, laid out dead on the road with their heads broken and things spilling out of them.

He had lost other friends like Kioso. There were other streetboys he had known better, for even longer, who had disappeared. But this was different. It wasn't about things that happened around him. And it was in that other place out there, with that white man, that lorry they jumped onto, and him running away, leaving Kioso. He never used to cry about things like that. He used to cry about his father, but nobody else. But he cried though that night in the woman's house.

He understood the arrangement with the police. He should wait for them to telephone the woman and tell her about Kioso coming back. But he didn't want to stay at the woman's house, and he didn't think why. He just stole some food from the cupboard and a pair of old sandals that belonged to one of her children, and went out the door.

He walked for a long time that night. His feet were still sore, but he managed to walk all the way across the city to the harbour. He avoided the other people and cars moving about. The avenue was quiet and warm, and he passed some skinny prostitutes who asked, laughing, if he wanted to taste something sweet. At last he turned into the harbour road and crept across to the ship hull, crawled inside, lay down and slept.

He slept long and hard that night, not moving at all. The plank under his back was the same it had always been, the creaking boards he squeezed through were the same too, and there were even old fruit peels and bits of rubbish from when he, Kioso, and the other boys had slept there some time before. And Kioso's name was still scratched into the wood, as were the names of all the other kids who had ever stayed there. Ali, Mika, Heriel, Kioso, Moses.

It was late when Moses woke the next morning, and it was already hot by the time he emerged from the ship hull. He walked to the market past the old homeless men, the orange vendor with the clubfeet, who waved a finger at him, and Prosper, who eyed him as he went along.

He made his way through the market, past the fruit stalls, the meat stalls, the beans and spices and rice, the cooking pots and sarongs, past the sisal mats and the women selling powders of medicine in old *Konyagi* bottles. He gazed at the young men selling radios and cassettes and fancy new things, but kept going.

Moses walked all the way back across town to Mama Tesha's house. He asked her if she had heard from the police, and she asked him if he had seen her daughter's sandals. Then she looked down at them on Moses's feet, and laughed. But she stopped laughing, and told Moses, her hand on his shoulder, that she hadn't heard anything yet. And Moses walked back to the harbour. No Kioso. Still gone up in the forest.

The next day he went back again, and again, no luck, no call, no Kioso. And the next day, the same. For weeks, it became a sort of routine for him: wake up in the morning, walk to the market, beg for change, steal some food along the way, walk across town to Mama Tesha's house, ask about Kioso, walk back, sleep in the ship hull. He didn't wander at night any more.

In the city, people went to certain places at the same time every day. They rested or ate in the same places at the same hour. Shops opened and closed the same way every day, except Saturdays and Sundays. Some things were different: the fish didn't always arrive in the market, and sometimes when the moon was gone, the Muslims called the month Ramadan and refused to eat in the daylight. And even that was a routine.

But the concept of routine had never before existed for Moses. When something happened, it happened, and when an opportunity came up, he took it. Otherwise, he slept under trees, sniffed glue now and then, smoked a joint or cigarette if somebody gave it to him, watched the world as it went on around him, and wanted things. Things: money, watches, cars, food, stuff. But since he had returned to Dar, he had developed this routine of waiting for Kioso.

He also didn't hang around with the other streetkids as much as he used to, except when they all went to beg on the street, and when they slept together in the ship hull. One night, the others asked him about Kioso, and he told them. They listened and ate what food they had, and went to sleep thinking about another boy gone from the street.

One day, though, this routine took a twist. Moses walked through the market and started to make his way to Mama Tesha's house. He passed the orange vendor with the clubfeet and snatched a piece of fruit for his journey, just like he did almost every day.

But this time, the man grabbed him. Just like the old white man taking Kioso's arm, this old man had his.

"Now I got you!" The old man laughed.

At first, Moses was surprised at how quickly the man moved for a cripple. He was puzzled, not scared, as the man kept laughing.

"You think I never could see you coming, boy? You think I'm just an old cripple sitting here, not knowing what's going on around me? Look around, little child! See all these people selling things, stealing things, running this way and that. Why do you think I'm still around? Because I watch everything and know it all too. That's right."

Moses just stared at the man and listened. The man laughed again, keeping his grip on Moses's arm, pointing and waving with the other hand as he continued his lecture.

"And you don't think I could have one of these boys around here take you for a beating, because you steal my fruit every day? You know that I know *everybody* in this market? I know everybody, everywhere. Every single last one of them, from the beggars to the thieves to the big men coming down in their fancy Mercedes-Benzes, even little *panyas* like you.

"I was here before they even built this big thing here, and that over there—when there was just that mosque over the street, that *duka* there, and just a line of us with our stands selling our things. Nothing else, and not you either, you kids running all over."

The man kept laughing as if he'd been playing a game for a long time and had just won. Moses still said nothing, standing awkward and dumb in the old man's grasp.

"I want you to sit down here, child. I won't hurt you."

Moses sat on a crate by the old man.

"What's your name?"

"Moses."

"Why do you keep stealing my fruit?"

"I'm hungry."

"Why do you never steal anyone else's fruit? Like Hadija over there. Or any of those other people. In fact, you're my best customer, except you never pay for any of it."

"I don't know."

"No, no. You tell me. Why do you steal only *my* fruit?"

Moses looked around, then told the truth. "You are old. You can't run. You got clubfeet."

"Does that make my fruit sweeter? It must be that I have the best fruit. You just say it's the best because I'm old and got clubfeet."

Moses looked at the man.

"Got clubfeet, but I caught you now, didn't I?"

The old man erupted into laughter once again, and Moses also started a hesitant laugh. The old man gave him an orange and took one off the stand for himself. They peeled their fruit and started to eat.

"That is sweet! The sweetest orange in the whole market, says this boy Moses right here!" the old man shouted out to the marketplace. Some of the other vendors started to look and point and chuckle at the old man.

"Listen, child. If you want fruit—even the sweetest fruit—you can have it. As much as you want, as much as your little *panya* mouth can hold. But you help me. Be here in the morning, early. I may be able to catch little rats like you by the arm, but I can't lift those sacks off the truck, and the boy who was working for me left. I'll give you food and some change. But you got to work, and you got to stay away from those older boys, and you got to stay out of the big roads. You'll just get yourself killed."

"How much money will you give me?"

"Now listen to you talking like a businessman. I'll give you something. You don't be picky, child."

"Okay. I can do that. I can be here."

"Good then. Early."

"Can I go now?"

"Well, yes."

"I have to go somewhere, but I will be here tomorrow."

"All right, then. See you tomorrow, Moses."

Moses grabbed an orange from the stand and headed off to Mama Tesha's house before it got dark.

Moses showed up for work the next day, and helped the old man unload his fruit. And the old man gave him food and a decent bit of change. So Moses got a new routine. He spent his mornings working and his afternoons checking with Mama Tesha, but no word came of Kioso.

He thought again of his father and farms, but these ideas seemed even further away. What did seem real and recent was Kioso. He was still in his head. When someone yelled at him or a car hooted loudly, or when he saw fights at the market, he thought of Kioso. That one image stuck in his head: Kioso hanging motionless and limp in the man's grasp, as he ran away.

He had relived his run through the forest many times over the weeks and months since his return to Dar, and always the same things popped into his head: looking down at his foot with no sandal and walking across the field of dead maize stalks in the small light of night. Other times, though, he would sit and think of Kioso's body.

Guilt and worthlessness still lived strong in Moses's stomach. He had never been responsible for anything or anyone in his life, but for those two days, he had the job of taking care of Kioso. Maybe because Kioso was small. Or because Moses had been on the streets for longer. Either way, it had happened that way. And Moses had left him.

Over the months that Moses worked for the orange vendor, he saw the bully-crook Prosper most days. Prosper didn't seem to grow up like the more successful crooks in town did. He had his big days—like when he showed up with some stolen radios. And he had his friends around him to tell him things were cool. He even had some new clothes, fancy shoes from America, sunglasses and all. But he was starting to lose something.

As Moses spent more time at the market, he watched the mighty Prosper, who had so often haunted his occasional visits to the market, degenerate into a lazy kid too old for petty theft. And his friends started to leave him. One left for a real job down by the docks. Moses saw another one hawking plastic things by the road, and he no longer looked like trouble. Another landed in jail for a few nights before going back to Kenya. And they were replaced by two or three younger, more stupid assistants, who spent more time admiring girls and new watches than finding ways to get money.

And every day Prosper watched Moses at work with the orange vendor. He watched him laugh at the old man's stories. He watched him listen to the old man, laughing as he waved his hands about as if to compensate for the lameness of his legs. He watched Moses and the market itself. He saw new big men coming. He saw the idiots hanging around him. He saw things change, people growing older and taller than him. He felt like they were all moving forward on a train and he was just standing in the same place.

Even some of the guys who used to be at his side had something now. He would scoff at them in public, mock their pathetic jobs, ask them if they felt big selling those plastic things by the road. He'd laugh out loud at them, but he couldn't shake the vacant feeling in his body. Even that streetkid with the orange vendor, he thought, had some money now. Something, at least.

Moses also watched the people: the other streetkids, the men delivering things in trucks, the taxi drivers, the young men like Prosper hanging around. Moses knew that Prosper was eyeing him, and Moses kept his distance.

"I need to go early today," Moses asked the old man one day. "That okay? I'll pack up first."

"What? Are you already tired of my stories, boy?"

"Just need to go."

"Go on, then."

It was hot. Moses walked to the other side of the street in the shade, where the younger guys sold the cool things, and where Hussein with the skinny head and the Muslim cap sold cassettes.

"Hi, Hussein."

"Eh, *vipi* Moses! Come here, little man. Listen to this."

Moses went around to the back of Hussein's small shack and stepped inside. Music was blaring from a big radio, and cassettes were packed tight into every bit of space. There were some soda bottles on the floor and cigarettes and an ashtray, and Hussein smiling like he always did.

"Here, listen to this, little man. This is something real good."

Hussein turned the volume dial up slowly, grinning and shaking his head.

"Man, this is the new thing. Radi Bundala again. 'The Master.' This is his new song. Listen here, kid. C'mon and move like you're in one of those discos on Mkwepu Street. Dancing with some nice big pretty woman. Like this, little man."

"I can dance, man. Radi's cool."

Moses just sat and moved his head to the music, the Master calling out, watching Hussein shake his skinny legs, his skinny head and flop his arms up and down his sides. Moses rested his chin in his hands and his elbows on his knees and listened.

Ujamaa, sisters!
Together, brothers!
We walk!
We fight!
Together, brothers
We unite!

"That's loud. Cool, *kabisa*."

Hussein lit a cigarette and blew a cloud of smoke.

"I need to go."

"You'll miss the next song. It's good," said Hussein, blowing more smoke at the ceiling. "That's the one they're playing on the radio all the time now. The Master's doing a concert at the stadium in a few months. It will be cool. I'm going."

Moses stepped out of Hussein's stall, heading towards the big road to get to Mama Tesha's house, singing the song in his head. He imagined the band playing their instruments, Radi singing, the guitars and the drums. And all the people watching, dancing, filling the stadium.

Moses made his way past the big shops and away from the market. The cars were loud and busy and he walked through the fumes and heat and yelling people.

When Prosper grabbed him, he tried to run, but it was too late. Prosper pulled him into an alleyway and pushed him against a wall. He looked around to see if anyone was near.

"I know that old man gives you money, little rat," he said, slapping Moses in the face.

"I don't have any today."

Prosper slapped him again and hit him in the stomach. He pushed him harder against the wall and punched Moses on the cheek, on the bone. Moses squirmed, trying to get free, but Prosper hit him three more times in the face, hard blows to his eye and lip.

"If I ask for money, you give money," he said, pushing Moses to the ground.

Prosper left, and Moses stayed on the floor of the alley. He could see rubbish around him and water coming out of one of the buildings. Both human and dog shit lay about. Some was on his arm. Plastic bags, shreds of soggy cardboard, papaya skins and fishbones were scattered around him. Moses lifted himself to sit against the wall. His back and side and bottom were wet from the garbage and shit and water, and he sat there in it, holding his face in his hands.

He could see the big road from where he was slumped in the dark alleyway. Out there it was sunlight and cars and people and dust and fumes. It was hot out there, but he was wet and dirty and his cheek throbbed with pain. Moses rested the back of his head against the wall, one hand over his sore cheek, the other on the wet ground.

He did not make it to Mama Tesha's that day. He did not want to be around anyone. He just wanted to go back to the ship hull. And he did not want to run into Prosper again.

The next morning he didn't go to the orange vendor, and he stayed away from the market. Only after a few days did he go back. The old man didn't ask him why he had not showed up the days before. Instead, he touched the boy's cheek and said little, and Moses went about his work. And Prosper hung around.

Prosper found him again that day and Moses gave him his money. The next few days were fine, but then he got beaten again. Moses tried running once, and got away. The next time he tried, he got another beating and his money taken.

Prosper didn't have his assistants around him when he mugged Moses or beat him. He was always alone. He always found Moses somewhere away from the market, away from his friends, Hussein, the orange vendor, from anyone who could see him. It was as if he didn't want to be seen doing something so low.

And the next day, it happened.

"Well, good morning, Moses," the old man greeted him. "I got some tea. But first help those drivers with my sacks, and get the stall ready."

Moses unloaded some sacks. Mainly the small ones, as some were bigger than he was. In fact the whole job was fit for a person twice Moses's size, and there wasn't very much he could do except run errands for the old man, move smaller sacks around and arrange the oranges and other fruit neatly on the stall.

Moses did not see Prosper until late that day when the old man was preparing to go home. Moses was waiting for him to finish and pay him some change, and then he would help him hobble his way to a *matatu* to go home.

But then Prosper showed up.

"Old man, why are you helping this *shenzi* rat?"

The old man rose with difficulty and looked at Prosper. He actually appeared tall when he stood, but was unsteady.

He leaned on his cane and squinted his eyes with an anger that Moses had not before seen. But before the old man could speak, Prosper slammed both hands against the old man's chest, sending him backwards onto the crates, the fruits spilling and rolling with him. Prosper remained still, somewhere between rage and disbelief at himself. His jaw was clenched as he stood looking down at the old man, who lay where he had fallen, and did not move.

When Moses hit Prosper in the back of the head with the shovel, Prosper's knees fell in like the old man's had. Blood came from his head. The market fell silent. Hussein ran up, looked down at Prosper, and then told Moses that he should drop that shovel and run and never come back.

And that's what Moses did.

Chapter 3

Is the old man dead? Is Prosper dead? Did I kill him? Now I can't ever go back. Did his friends see? They'll get me, and Prosper will get me too, if he isn't dead. Or I'll go to prison and they'll keep me there in those bad places where they got you all shut up in small rooms and you get beaten. Some go to that other place for kids, but Mika told me that's no better. All those kids and the bigger ones beat on you, just like on the streets. Except you can't run anywhere.

I can't even go to the harbour. Prosper knows I stay around there, already got me there once. Need to get to another part of town. Somewhere far. Some place where I won't get found.

I don't even know what happened after I left. Hussein just said run. Did the police come? Maybe they're now looking all over for me. I need to get on a matatu *or something. Get far from here. There's one.*

A *matatu* driver pulled over.

"Where you going, kid?"

"I don't have money, but I need a lift. Please." Moses slapped the door, but the driver sped off.

Another *matatu* pulled up and Moses asked again. The driver eyed him with caution.

"Okay. Get in. Sit back there."

Moses sat in the back while the *matatu* drove further and further away from the market area. He got off at the stadium and walked across the empty ground in front of it. He crawled behind some broken boards and wire where he could be out of sight. He stayed there for a little while, but it did not feel right, did not feel safe. So he left.

He began to walk to Mama Tesha's house, the one place he knew where nobody could find him. It was getting dark as he walked up to her house. The rooms inside were dark, and the small dirt street in front of it was empty. Quiet.

Moses knocked on the door softly for a long time. He was nervous, but had been there before, many times, and the kids and the husband knew him, and were used to seeing him come around.

But today, nobody. Moses banged on the door, louder and now more urgently. He turned to look at the street, and then banged again and peered through a window. When he realised there was no chance, no one at home, he sat for a moment on the ground in front of the door. He looked at the sky getting darker in this strange part of town, and thought of Mama and her family, feeling like they had somehow abandoned him.

Moses spent another night walking the streets. It reminded him of the first night he had left Mama Tesha's house. It was dangerous to walk the streets at night, and he knew it. He knew he should just get into some safe place and stay put. But every time he crawled inside somewhere, he felt trapped. Out here on the street, he thought, at least he could run.

Moses walked down the big empty street, black and dark like the sky. He saw the big empty shops that looked so different during the day. He watched a couple of rats fighting and cats digging in rubbish containers, and remembered Prosper beating him for the first time in the alley. He walked on and down towards Mkwepu Street where the discos were, but thought again about all the people there, and decided to stay clear.

It was late and the skinny prostitutes were out. Always waiting and acting like the day was just beginning. He walked over and stood near the women. He feared crowds, but he also feared the emptiness of the streets, and he felt better standing near these women, whom he knew would not harm him.

He watched them talk, lean against the wall, smoke. He saw them stand up straight and call out to men and passing cars, and then slouch down when the cars kept driving. They sat on crates and old stools, just like anyone else. They even acted like little girls sometimes, he thought, laughing and chatting and listening to the one tall woman who talked the most.

A car stopped. One of the women got in, and it drove off. Another just got taken over to a field near the road, and she came back after a few minutes. The rest stood or sat and watched the traffic and the few people still walking around.

Later, when business got slow, they called him over and talked to him, and gave him a cigarette. The tall one gave him a free touch. She put his little grubby hand up her shirt, and the others laughed as his hand just sat there on her big warm soft tit. But one woman did not laugh. Moses was embarrassed and skulked off to the side to sit on a crate. The woman who did not laugh came and sat down next to him.

"What's your name?"

"Moses."

"Hi. I'm Grace."

They sat for a while, watching the road. A car passed, slowed, the driver's head turning to look at the women, and then it drove on.

"What are you doing here, boy?" Grace glanced over at the other women as she spoke. "Don't you have anywhere you can go? Not even some place?"

"Not today."

She did not say anything else, but sitting next to her felt comforting. She seemed different from the other women. She wore the same clothes as the others, but she did not talk like the others, or chase after cars, or walk in that funny prostitute way like the others. He had known many *changudoa* in his short life, mainly the ones down by the harbour, but she was different. She did not laugh a lot, but when she did, she did not seem like a prostitute as he knew them to be, but more like the women selling things at the market.

As it got very late, the women went off to their various homes to sleep away the few remaining hours of the night. Grace also rose to leave.

"Bye, Grace."

"Bye, Moses."

She started off down the road, but stopped after a few tired steps and turned back to Moses.

"Are you going to sit here all night?"

Moses did not answer. He actually didn't know where he was going or what he would do once everyone had left.

"Look, if you stay here, one of the gangs will come and beat you *kabisa.*" Moses kept looking at her as if to say, "Well, I got no choice." Grace hesitated.

"*Mimi kichaa kweli,*" she said, shaking her head at herself. "Come with me. I'm going home."

They started down the street together. Moses was astonished that this woman would actually take him into her house. He knew that if he were a prostitute, he would not invite some dirty streetkid into his house.

The two made an unlikely pair as they walked along, the prostitute in high heels and a black skirt cut high on her thigh, and Moses in his usual stained, torn shirt and stolen sandals.

They arrived at her room. It was a shack, but it had sturdy walls and a door that locked, and it felt like a safe place to be. She had a bed, a hotplate, some clothes hanging from nails on the door, a little table, and a kerosene lantern that she lit once they were inside. Moses looked at her clothes and her fancy work shoes. Next to them were old sandals just like his.

She told him to turn around as she took off her working clothes, put on an old shirt, and wrapped herself in a sarong.

"That woman gave you one free touch tonight, but you are not looking at me. You're still just a kid."

She smiled, but looked tired. She put a blanket on the floor and told Moses to lie down and sleep there. She told him he had better not take anything, that the door was locked and that she had the key, and that there would be no place for him to run anyways.

She went outside to bathe and Moses stayed inside on her floor in the dim light. He lay down with his blanket, finally realising how tired he was. He waited until Grace returned to the room. He watched her come inside, moving slowly. He could see the outline of her breasts as they sagged in the thin shirt she wore for bed.

She lifted the glass of the lantern, shortened the wick, blew out the flame and lay down on her bed. Moses fell asleep.

✽

Moses woke up thinking about Grace's tits. He relived, moment by unsure moment, how the other prostitute had taken his hand up into her shirt, and the way she and the others laughed. How warm and mysterious she had felt. He wondered what Grace's tits would feel like.

He looked over at her sleeping on the bed. Her lips were softly closed. Her eyes looked peaceful. She held the bedsheet clenched up to her chin with one hand, the other tucked under her neck. Some light was coming through the small window and across part of her bed.

Moses thought of other people waking up, Prosper too, wherever he stayed. Moses imagined him in a room with other men around him, making a plan to find him. In his head, he created their discussions about the various and many ways to beat him, what they would do first, and where they would take him afterwards.

He felt edgy, but knew that it was still early, and that when Grace woke up, she would make tea, and he would probably get some. So he watched her and looked around her room and waited for her to wake up. Tacked on the wall was a photo of some people, her family maybe, standing in a row looking nervous, as if having a photo taken was a special experience. Behind them were trees and a field. It looked like nothing he had seen around Dar es Salaam. More like the country he had seen when he and Kioso had jumped off the lorry. There was also a necklace of plastic beads hanging from a nail in the wall, a cross on the wall as well, and some old magazines on the floor by the bed.

When she woke up, she boiled tea, and Moses had three cups. Her hair was a wiry spasm, upright, but at odd angles, so she pulled it back and under a scarf. She sat on the bed with her back against the wall. Her sarong was wrapped and tucked nicely around her body, and her shirt was loose and low. Moses looked at her tits and thought again of the night before when he had touched the other woman, and how these seemed different and low. When Grace leaned forward to pour more tea, he could see them hanging like large, smooth aubergines.

Later, Moses went to check Mama Tesha's house, and again there was nobody home. He waited around in that part of town, checked again, and then walked back to Grace's house. She was still there, reading her magazines in her sarong, and Moses stayed with her until the late afternoon, when they ventured out together. He was surprised that she tolerated him around, but she didn't seem to mind.

She took him to a busy shack selling tripe soup and rice, and they ate sitting across from one another. She watched him as he ate, lost in thought, as if he resembled someone she knew, a younger brother perhaps. Or as if he made her think of a place, a person, or a time in her life when things were different.

After they had eaten, they returned to her house and spent more time relaxing. Moses looked at her magazines, at the pictures of musicians and famous men and women all dressed up and looking important. Some of her friends came by and stayed for a few hours, chatting and drinking tea. After it got dark, Grace bathed outside again and began her preparations for the evening.

Moses joined her and the other prostitutes at the same corner, and spent another night with Grace. The next day and night were the same, and the following morning, Moses finally found Mama Tesha.

"Well, look who is coming by now. You still owe me a pair of sandals, you know?"

"Hi, Mama."

Moses stood looking at her, then at the street, then back at her, as if waiting for something.

"I haven't heard anything about your friend, my child. I'm sorry. You know, it's been a long time. I have also been away."

Moses nodded and still waited.

"I have to go, Moses. I have to get to my shop now. Come, walk with me there."

She shut the door to her house, and the two started out along the street. Moses didn't talk much, and she told him about her trip with her family down the coast for the funeral of her husband's mother, and how hot it was, and how all they ever ate down there was fish.

"Here. Come in. You've never seen my shop before, have you? And don't touch my sandals, child."

Her shop was not as small as it appeared from the outside. It extended deep inside, and was stocked with food, clothes, footballs, nails, glue, all sorts of things. There was a storage room at the back and an enclosed courtyard with a toilet. Moses sat with her on stools behind the counter. She kept no lights on, and it was cool inside. Another boy was there, older than Moses, and he looked after most of the customers who came in. But it was still early, so Mama made tea, and the three of them drank and ate slices of bread with margarine.

The morning got late, and while the older boy was busy with a customer, Moses told Mama about the old man with the clubfeet and Prosper and the fight and Grace. Mama listened and cocked her eyebrow the way she always did when she found something interesting, out of place or wrong.

He told her he wanted to know what happened, but that he could never go back, even though he liked working for the old man. He asked her if he could work for her, just like he worked for the old man.

"I never stole anything from him and I was always there and helping him."

Mama looked down at Moses, wondering how best to say "no." She thought of excuses, that she just could not have a streetkid hanging around her shop. Simple as that. She looked down at him with her eyebrows together, crossed her arms and looked away, and then told him to go fetch something while she thought some more.

Moses jumped off his stool and went into the yard, and Mama called over the older boy and asked him what he thought. He also said "no" at first, then "no way, never," but then they discussed it. Moses came back.

"Listen here, child. I will let you help, but if you cause any *maneno*, then I will throw you out."

"Thank you, Mama."

"I'm saying, here's how it works. You help me out and I'll give you change and food to eat. You steal from me, and you'll get a real beating. And I'll bring the police and that other boy from the market that you're so scared of. Hear that?"

Moses nodded.

"Fine, then. But first you work to pay for your sandals. After that, you can get change."

The other boy in the shop was called Ali. He reminded Moses of Hussein from the market, but he wasn't as friendly. He was serious and as he did his work, he kept a watchful eye on Moses. Like Hussein, he liked his music, and played the old radio in the shop when Mama wasn't around. As soon as she would leave on an errand or to go home, Ali would turn up the music and sometimes smoke a cigarette.

That night they closed up the shop, and Moses sat on the small bench outside. Mama rushed off in a hurry for something she had to do, and Ali just locked up and walked off. Neither seemed to consider that Moses had nowhere to sleep. Moses sat on the bench and watched the people walking by. All the people going home at the end of the day, women carrying things in plastic bags. He looked at their bags and imagined what was inside each one—sugar, maize-meal, a packet of tea, soap. He watched others ride by on bicycles and small groups of Muslims going to the mosque in their clean white *kanzus*.

The street activities died down. It was a quieter street, not like those roads where the men sell street food at night and hair salons stay open late. This road got quiet, and soon it was empty except for Moses, who sat on the bench in the dark. He was hungry. He knew where to find food—back around the harbour and other places. But he did not leave. Instead, he curled up on the bench outside Mama's shop and slept hungry.

He woke for a few hours in the night and lay on his side looking across the road. He fell asleep again and woke in the morning to the sights and sounds of people coming from their homes and going to work or school. Moses watched three children his age in green school uniforms pass him chatting on their way to school. One was holding a book open as they walked, and the other two were leaning over him, looking at it. They did not notice Moses, but he watched them. He looked at one's watch and the other one's shoes. And he looked at the book. His eyes followed them until they were out of sight.

When Mama arrived, she looked with surprise at Moses on the bench. It was evident that he had slept there all night. She felt ashamed that she had so easily overlooked the fact that the boy had no place to sleep at night. So from that day on, Mama allowed him to sleep in the storage room behind the shop. It led to the enclosed courtyard area, and when she left, Mama would lock the whole place up with Moses inside. It was safe as could be, and at first he liked it.

He would sit in the open area at night and burn charcoal on the small grill and cook *ugali* and sing to himself the songs he heard on the radio. He would think about the day and the different customers in the shop, about the kids who played football in the street, about Prosper and Kioso and Ali, and quite often about Grace's tits. He would wonder what Mama's tits looked like and then laugh. He would think of the other boys in the ship hull and miss them and go to sleep feeling lonely.

He also thought about Grace's room and the cross on her wall and the photograph of the people standing in front of a field. Her family. He remembered the fields he ran through when he escaped from the old white man. Those events seemed further away now. The episodes with Prosper and the orange vendor were more recent in his mind. Kioso was there too, but that memory was less sharp.

There was a customer who came to the shop once a week, whom Mama treated like an old friend. His name was George. He was a funny-looking bald man with hair only around his ears, thick glasses and purply-black skin. One time he bought all the footballs in the shop. He blew one up right there and tossed it to Moses and invited him into the street to play. They kicked for a while, then the man laughed and paid Mama and waved and got into his truck and went off.

Moses passed his days this way for some time—helping in the shop during the day, sleeping in the storeroom each night. He had never done anything like this for so long. Like with the orange vendor, it was a routine of sorts, and Moses wasn't very good at routine. But he continued, because for the time being at least, the security of it all felt good to him.

He also started saving a bit of money. Never before in his life had Moses saved anything. It had never occurred to him, never been an option to consider, but now it was a novelty. Every week, he would take some of the coins Mama gave him and hide them in a jar that he wedged into a small crevice in the storeroom. It was almost like a game. Over time, he saved a fair amount of money, and there was only one way to spend it.

"Ali. You going to Radi's concert tomorrow?"

"*Kabisa.* It's going to be *safi*."

"Me too."

"Ha! How are you going to do that?"

"I got money. Some money. Maybe it is enough to buy a ticket?"

Moses went to the storeroom and returned with his jar of coins.

"You saved all that money?"

"How much do I need?"

Ali looked suspiciously at Moses, then reached for the jar of coins. He held it up.

"I'll help you count it. Come sit over here."

They poured the coins out onto the counter, separated the different-sized coins into piles, and counted them.

"Not bad. Seems like enough to get a ticket. Maybe he'll play *Vipi Young Brother* for you! Everybody will go crazy when he plays that."

The next day Ali called Moses over.

"Come on over here, little Radi, little man. You can come with me to the concert. We'll all go together. You and me and John and Yusuph."

"Cool. Thanks." Moses smiled.

Ali looked down at the little kid and his pathetic clothes. He had never really noticed Moses's clothes before. He was used to seeing streetkids in rags and had gotten used to seeing Moses that way. But at that moment, he looked at him differently, the coins he had saved spread out on the counter, Moses smiling about going to see the concert.

In the late afternoon, the hot air was still heavy on the streets. The shop was stuffy and humid. Ali had gone home and returned to the shop with his two friends. They looked smart in their best clothes, their shoes polished and their hair combed. The smell of Yusuph's perfume filled the shop as he walked in.

"Hey, kid, take this. Your luck today."

He handed Moses a shirt, purple with yellow around the collar and wide cuffs and buttons going down the front.

"It's big, but so is the one you always wear. You'll look like one of Radi's guitar players."

Ali's friends laughed, and Yusuph reached in the plastic bag by his side and pulled out a pair of trousers.

"And try this, little man."

Moses dressed and looked into a hand-mirror that Ali held up for him. The clothes were far too large, but he rolled up the pant-legs and the sleeves on the shirt, and looked at himself from the front and then from the side, sticking his chest out and putting on a serious face. He took a comb and fixed his hair and licked his fingers and wiped places on his face. Then he stepped back and looked at himself again, from the side and then from the front.

"And for the girls, a little of this."

Yusuph sprayed Moses with his perfume, and the three stepped back and judged Moses with approval.

"Look at you. The kid Moses. Now you're ready, little man."

The four of them walked to the stadium, strutting slow, ready for the big show. Moses had never had friends like Ali, Yusuph, and John, people dressed up with money to spend.

At the stadium, they pushed through the crowd of people at the front gate trying to get inside. Moses saw other kids his age, going in, dressed up smart, and then other kids from the street just lying on the grass outside, knowing they would never get inside. He looked over at them as he entered, but he didn't recognise any of them.

Inside, it was big. Concrete steps rose all around a great field, and thousands of people sat or stood, screaming back and forth to each other. Down on the field, equipment was stacked and scattered about, and the people standing down there were pushing up tight against one another.

He and Ali and John and Yusuph climbed high up on the concrete steps, nearly to the top, and looked down over the crowd. Moses heard the sound of the guitars and drums. Twenty or so men and women were poised on the huge black stage, dressed in brilliant, colourful *kangas*.

Then Radi came out. Moses recognised him by his dreadlocks and his round sunglasses. Radi screamed out to the crowd, and then the musicians and dancers began.

He sang about women and men beating them and how that was bad. Moses heard songs about politicians and money and life, and heard him yell out things about Mozambique and Uganda and Kenya, and all sorts of other places he didn't know about. Radi sang about unity and sadness and poverty and home. And all the time, the men banged loud on drums and the guitars kept playing and the brightly dressed women kept dancing.

The music stopped after a while, and Ali told Moses that it would start again after half an hour.

"Let's go walk around."

"Look at some girls, like that one there with the nice *wowowo*."

"That's big. That's nice."

"Moses, look at that girl!"

"Cool."

"Come on, let's go walk."

They walked even higher up in the crowded stadium until they stood on the highest step. Then they walked along to the other side of the stadium, Yusuph, John, and Ali talking about girls the whole way. Moses listened, nodding at what they said. He thought of Grace, wondering if she would be at the concert, but then he realised she was probably working on the street for the men.

When the music started again, they descended down further into the crowd, and Radi sang out:

Look over here, child.
I have a message for you.
You are trying to make it,
But you never get it.
You walk here, on this road.
You don't get money.
You don't get anything.
Listen to me child.
There is nothing for you in this town.

Yusuph yelled out and whistled and waved his arms, along with the crowd. All the people jumped and danced and screamed, and the crowd got thicker and more people pushed up close to them. Moses strained to see over the other people, so Ali and John lifted him into the air.

And in their arms high up in the air, Moses felt like the biggest man in the stadium. He felt that Radi could see him there. Moses laughed and screamed and raised his arms, and the crowd cheered him on, girls too, pointing and yelling out to him. It was the greatest moment he had ever had.

Then he saw Prosper. When he looked over to his left, he caught sight of Prosper, surrounded by his friends, staring at him. Prosper started to push through the crowd towards him.

Moses slapped Ali and John to let him down. He jumped out of their arms like a squirming cat and squeezed through the dancing bodies. Ali and his friends hardly noticed and kept dancing. Moses ran and pushed through the crowd, with Prosper chasing him.

Prosper lunged for Moses, grabbing his shirt and ripping it. He kept pulling, but Moses wriggled free of the shirt, and then he darted through the crowd and ran. Prosper kept after him, shirt in hand, and then when Moses was too far ahead to catch, Prosper held the shirt up over his head for Moses to see, like a prize.

Moses ran shirtless through the crowd, found his way to the gates and ran out and down the avenue. When he finally stopped running, he was far away, but he could still hear the music, which made him feel too close. He walked on quickly, feeling where Prosper's fingernails had scraped his back. He thought of what Ali was going to say about him losing his fancy purple shirt.

When he arrived at Mama Tesha's house, he banged on the door. The husband opened it and stood in the doorway, looking at Moses.

"Why don't you have a shirt on?"

Moses did not answer, but slipped past the man and went to Mama and told her about the concert. Her husband listened for a few moments and then shut the door and went into the other room. Mama took Moses to the bathroom and ordered one of her children to pour some warm water into a bucket for him. The other kids watched from the door, peering inside at Moses.

"Again? I say, this boy is no good, always beating on you. Where's Ali?"

"At the stadium."

"Where were they?"

"I ran."

"This boy is bad, really. Now, you just stay in here and clean yourself up and I'll be just outside when you're finished."

She closed the door and Moses stood in front of the mirror. He saw himself there and did not move. The bucket of water was at his feet and there was dirt on the floor of Mama's nice bathroom. He looked in the mirror at his face and chest and pants and sandals. His eyes squinted and his mouth opened and he cried, standing there with his arms hanging down at his sides. His crying was noiseless and breathless. Just his wide-open mouth, tears and twisted face.

Mama opened the door and came inside, closing the door behind her. Her movements were slow. She sat on the toilet seat with her legs pressed together and her elbows resting on her lap. Moses looked at her with his arms dangling, like someone wet and cold, until Mama took a towel and wrapped him in it, and brought him into her arms, and hugged him like nobody had done for a long time.

Chapter 4

When the rainy season began, the streets turned from dust into mud. Ditches grew deep, as if an invisible army were digging its trenches, and giant puddles formed in the road where before only shallow depressions had existed. Cars mostly drove slowly through them, but sometimes a truck would hit one too fast and splash the passersby.

It rained during the day and during the night too, coming down loud on the iron-sheet roof of the shop. People would hang around the shop longer than usual, sitting on the benches by the entrance and looking at the sky with their elbows on their knees and chins resting on hands. Days passed, with less talk than usual. People would think their thoughts looking at the rain in the street and at the sky above. It felt like the time near the end of a long walk, when people keep to themselves, waiting for it to end.

As for Moses, he was still there. He went on working for Mama and staying in the back of the shop. He missed his friends from the harbour a lot, and thought of them more often than before. He thought more often about Kioso too.

The bald man with glasses named George still came to Mama's shop every week, and every week he would joke with Moses or kick a football around the muddy street with him for a few minutes before driving back to wherever he came from. Moses would wave to him as he drove off, and then sit back down on the bench and watch the rain.

One time when the rain was really strong and blowing sideways, George stayed longer, sitting in the shop with Mama and drinking tea. He and Ali and Mama and Moses all sat there inside on the stools, talking about the noise of the rain hitting the roof and when it was going to stop.

"It's also raining up in Bangata," said George. "Good for the farmers, finally. You know they suffered a long dry season. Cattle were dying all over. In the bush, the Maasai were dragging them by their horns to waterholes. Maize all dried up too."

"Well, they should plant their maize in this road here. Too much water. And even more in my shop from everybody bringing it in on their shoes."

"What do you think, Moses?"

"Yes?"

"Look at all this rain."

Moses nodded, but did not respond.

"We need it. Especially up in Bangata."

Moses didn't say anything, and George paused to think. He looked down at his boots, hard and leather and waterproof, and at his new pants, and then at his Land Rover outside. It belonged to the school he ran, but only he used it, so it felt more or less like his own car. He looked back at Moses.

"Moses, have you ever been out of Dar?"

Moses looked at him, and then at Mama, and back through the door at the rain coming down.

"Yes."

"Where?"

"Don't know." He paused. "Just went once."

"I live out in the country, you know. Well, at least the country when compared to Dar es Salaam. Near a small village. It's different." He shifted in his seat. "Have you ever been in school, Moses?"

"No."

"How old are you?"

"Eleven now."

"Never been in any school, huh?"

"No."

"Can you read or write?"

"No." Moses spoke to the floor.

George leaned back and crossed his arms. "Well, would you want to go to a school?"

Moses looked at him and at Mama and then at Ali, who was busy looking at a cassette he had bought and wasn't even listening.

"Yes." He thought it might be what he wanted, but truthfully he did not know. School had never been an option, something to like or dislike, to want or not.

"Did Mama ever tell you I have a school? Up in the country, for kids who have no family. Like you, no? Do you have family?"

Moses did not answer. He did not look away or at the man or at anything. He was frozen in the moment, trying to think of the correct answer.

"I don't have family."

The man looked over at Mama Tesha, then hunched down closer to Moses.

"Would you want to come to my school? It's far from here, but there are other kids like you there, and it's a nice place. We have classes and we play football too. And maybe you can come back here with me sometimes when I buy my supplies, and you can see Mama."

"What do you think, Moses?" Mama asked.

Moses did not answer and looked outside, as if he wanted to get away. He thought of the ship hull and his friends there. He thought about the man's school and his offer, but mainly about his question about Moses's family. He saw the rain falling more lightly, and people just like them sitting in the shop across the street, also looking out their door. And he thought about all the places he had been in the past few years, and how he had ended up where he was.

Mama spoke. "George, why don't I talk about it with Moses. And we can discuss it with you next week when you come back to town."

"Yes, that is a good idea. You can talk about it."

George stood and looked outside. He put on his hat, and walked over to Moses, putting his hand on the boy's head.

"Rain's letting up. Maybe I'll race to my truck before it starts again. Thank you for the tea, Mama. And Moses, you think about it, talk with Mama Tesha. And we can discuss it again when I come back."

George stepped out of the door. "*Kwaheri*!" he yelled, waving as he ran across to his truck and jumped inside.

After several days, Moses and Mama discussed George's school again. They talked for a while, and Moses decided that he would go. But the next time George came back, Moses wasn't there. And the next time, he wasn't around either. It was as if he mysteriously went missing when George came around, as if he did not want to commit to the decision about school. He would think about when he had left Dar the last time: the fear, lost on the road, sleeping in ditches and under trees with all the strange noises at night. He would remember the dead snake they had found, and the grey Peugeot, the old white man emerging and squatting with his hand out, telling them to come to his house. He would remember the man's yellow teeth.

On the days that George came by, Moses ventured further than usual from Mama's shop, returning only after George had left. He stayed clear of the market and the harbour, even though something inside pulled him back. He even dreamed about the ship hull, laughing there with Mika and Kioso and the other streetkids. Talking, sleeping, playing, eating food they had gotten. Moses had been on his own for a long time now, without his pack, his friends.

He would loop around the city centre, avoiding the market, and walk far out on the other side of the main harbour, where the buildings spanned out low. It would take him a few hours, and sometimes it would be raining, but he would still go there to sit by the smaller harbour where the shallow dhows came ashore with fish.

Sitting there, he would feel as if he were in another city, another place altogether, with no way he could be seen by anyone he knew. It felt good in one way and lonely in another. The dhows would come ashore, washing gently up onto the sand. Fish would be thrown from their decks, and the fishermen would nod at him or just leave him be. They would pull their cloth sails down and drag their boats further up onto the sand and take the shirts that were wrapped around their heads and spread them on the cement by the road to dry. Boys on bicycles and old Swahili men in small trucks would come and buy the fish, and the fishermen would count their money slowly to be sure, and then nod and walk back to their boats.

Sometimes one or two of them would rest in the shade of the crumbling seawall, leaning against it, looking out. One might rub his shoulders, sore from pulling nets, but usually they would just sit tired and watch the water, thinking of the little money they made, or maybe of nothing at all.

Moses liked watching the fishermen. He would look at their lean muscles and their slow movements, which were strong and confident. One time, one of the men looked back at Moses. The man sat on the sand, his back and head resting against the wall, his arms on his knees. Moses had been watching him since he pulled his dhow ashore and threw dead fish onto the sand, handled the nets, gave some instructions to his younger deckhand, and then sat down against the wall. After some time, he noticed Moses watching him, and slowly turned his head towards him. And then he just looked at Moses, his tired eyes on the boy, a look without judgement or shame or pity. The man's expression seemed to be an explanation of his life, and perhaps of life as it was for all those living along the harbour, him and Moses all the same.

Moses returned several times to see the fisherman, always watching the one man in particular who would look back at him, but who never approached him. During his visits to the fishermen, he thought about George and his offer, and eventually he became comfortable with the idea. And after a few weeks, he stopped going to see the fishermen, and stayed at the shop, waiting for George to arrive. He gathered together the few things he had collected during his time at Mama's shop and waited for the man named George to come and take him away.

In George's white truck, Moses sat on his hands. He glanced over at the funny-looking man, at the balding crown of his head, polished like a river stone, and the white hairs spiralling in all directions from above his ears.

The rain was gone by now, back in hibernation somewhere in the sky, and Moses listened to the sounds of the dry, chalky stones hitting the floorboards as they drove. On a long road, and everything was different—the blue school shirt George had given him before they left Mama's, George's hand on the worn gear-stick, the thin trees flashing by on the arid wash of the landscape.

Moses's eyes were wide and alert, his lips together and still. He did not say anything. He was as nervous as he had expected. He did not look back. He only turned every now and then to look at something they passed—a dead hyena by the road, a row of women walking with baskets on their heads.

They stopped along the way to piss in the dust, watching it rise in clouds around their ankles. Moses could hear the vacancy of the bush around him, the silence. He heard no street, no voices. There were no men here. There was no ship hull to crawl inside, no Mama's shop. The quiet was enormous—broken only by the sound of their urine pattering in the dust.

When they climbed back in the truck, George took a jerrycan from the back and put it on Moses's seat for him to sit on, so he could see the countryside better.

After some hours, George slowed, grinding the gears, and stopped in front of a small restaurant. Two or three people sat about chewing on toothpicks and watching the road. George bought a packet of biscuits and two bottles of soda, which they ate and drank at a wooden table in the shade. It was quiet, and Moses looked out over the road, and at the few other shops and the petrol station. Other than that, it was just empty bush and fields, and he felt far from anything he had ever known.

The road continued as dusty as if the rains had never found their way there. Then, coming into the town of Bangata, the colours of the land changed from brown and grey into green and black. Moses stared at the fields with neat rows of maize and banana and coffee, the rivers in between, and the huge trees bending over the road.

George drove slowly through the town. Some people waved at him. Others stared. It was Saturday afternoon, and there was little activity. Moses watched people sitting outside cafés on plastic chairs, drinking tea or beer and eating meat and chicken and fried bananas. He saw the small park, and a couple of Indians standing outside their shops, and the market, which was empty except for some young men hanging around, just like in Dar.

After they passed through the town, George turned off the main road onto a smaller dirt road. Moses saw mountains in the distance that reminded him of the last time he was in the country with Kioso. It was not long before they arrived at a bare football field, and drove to where Moses could see some low, blue buildings and kids sitting under a big mango tree.

"Moses," declared George with a sweep of his arm, "This is my school. I am sure you're nervous. But the kids here are good kids, and I promise it's a nice place to be. It's Saturday, so I think we're playing a game of football today."

They stopped in front of the group of kids. A couple of men came over to greet George.

"Moses, this is Emmanuel, and this is Godson. They help me run the school."

"Hi, Moses. You are welcome."

The boys came to the vehicle to see the new kid. Moses was still sitting in the truck, and the kids stared and asked each other where they thought he was from. Moses looked at them and then away. George came around to Moses's door and opened it, and encouraged him to step out of the truck.

"All right, everybody, listen. This is Moses and he has come to stay with us. Say hello to him and welcome him to the Boys of the Future School."

"*Karibu* Moses!" the kids called out in unison. Then the man named Godson produced a football and kicked it towards the field.

"Time for football!" Godson sang out and the kids yelled back, and ran down to the field and started playing. Moses was standing there with George, watching the boys, when someone tapped on his shoulder. Moses turned.

"Kioso?"

❁

Moses and Kioso played football that afternoon before Moses was shown his bed in the dormitory. After George discovered the relationship between Kioso and Moses, he made sure their beds were next to each other. Yes, Moses felt relief. Yes, he felt immediate joy. He hugged Kioso with a grin across his face, so happy, truly happy, to know he was alive. Or was it because he did not have to feel guilt any more? The foundation for his suffering, searching, his trips to Mama's—it was guilt for having left Kioso to die. Guilt for killing Kioso by running away.

But his relief did not last long—soon he felt cheated. Kioso has been up here all this time, he thought. And nobody told me, and I'm getting beaten by Prosper and everything, and he's here in school playing football.

But Kioso was still the most familiar thing in that place. And in the evening, after supper, they sat outside on the grass.

"He just let you go? That old white man?"

"I woke up and he was asleep on the bed. The bottle and another one were on the floor. He was asleep with his legs hanging off the bed, so I left. Stayed in the forest that night, and the next day I got a lift to a town, and then another. Someone brought me up here. And I stayed."

"I tried to find you. When I was back in Dar, I asked every day if they found you. I did. Nobody told me you were here. That you were okay and in school up here. And after I left that night, I went to the police. They never told me anything about you. They said they would." Moses was desperate for Kioso to know of his efforts, to try to make Kioso understand that he had not abandoned him, that nobody had told him that he was safe.

Kioso rolled onto his back and looked up into the trees. "Did you see Mika and them?"

"They're all there. Nothing's changed. Except I hit Prosper one time and it made things bad."

"What? *Safi*!"

"Ha, it wasn't so cool. But I'll tell you about the Radi Bundala concert. *That* was *safi*!"

They talked for a long time, and Moses told a long story about Radi Bundala and the concert, but he didn't say any more about Prosper.

Chapter 5

For the next few months, Moses and Kioso stuck together. George understood them pretty well for a man who had never lived on the streets. But it was the country, so things were different for most of the kids. There were no girls. The other boys were from towns all over, but only Kioso and Moses came from a place as big as Dar. In the eyes of the other boys, it was an amazing thing to be from Dar. For them, the big city was an enormous mythical place on the other side of the world, and they always asked Moses to tell them about the harbour and the ocean and all the people.

The others were orphans, but very few of them had been streetkids. Unlike Moses, these kids had lost both parents. Moses still had a parent, a mother somewhere. And an uncle who had beaten him down. Now and then he would wonder why his mother had left him with such a bad man. What was wrong with her? Was she sick? He had memories of her, but they were only images, flashes of her washing, cooking, yelling. He had no memories of affection, only of fear and the belief that he was doing something wrong. She was always angry: at his father, at him, at everything. He would see insane women on the streets, abused, their clothes torn and eyes stoned, mumbling, and he would think of his mother.

This always made Moses feel different. And even though he resented Kioso, who had been safe all the time Moses had searched for him, he didn't know what it would be like if Kioso weren't there. Kioso was the only familiar thing, the only kid at the school who understood Dar and the way things were there.

Here it was a different world. On one side of town, the land rose up into mountains and lush farmland, eventually leading to high forests. On the other side, a dry expanse of acacia trees stretched into the distance to where a faint mountain range poked up along the horizon. Bangata was quiet. The school was quiet. They studied reading, writing, and maths, and they played football and did chores around the school.

Parts of Bangata and the school reminded Moses of his father's stories about the farms, but other things didn't seem to fit. The images in his head were right, but the feelings were different to the way he had imagined. He was finally surrounded by trees and farms and food, but it didn't feel like he thought it would. It felt empty, and his dreams of happily riding a bicycle around peaceful farms with his father were gone.

For the first couple of months, he more or less liked the luxuries of the school—the meals, the football, the comfortable beds, the hot water. But he struggled with the regimented ways of school life, and he was always uncomfortable with older men telling him things, whether they were right or wrong, for his benefit or not. Kioso felt the same way, but he was more used to the school, and, as always, he was more accepting of things than Moses. For Moses, there was always a nagging sense of urgency—he could never feel settled in a place so quiet and orderly.

Over the months, Moses learned to read a little, and he got to be a good footballer. But not much else changed. Another rainy season came and went. The days got hot in the afternoon, then cool at night, and then cool in the day and cold at night. Every once in a while, George would take him to Dar when he went to get supplies. Moses would see Ali and Mama Tesha and some of the regulars who lingered around the shop. He always hoped that George would drive out of town a different way and pass by the market or harbour, but he never did. Soon enough they would be on the dusty road heading back to Bangata.

He was caught stealing once from one of the workers. An old watch left by the sink in the washroom. George spoke to him for a long time. He was angry, but understanding. It was the only time Moses stole something at the school. He had not even wanted it. He didn't understand why he took it, if it was because the watch was just sitting there, or if he was simply trying to sabotage his situation.

Another time Moses disappeared, and George found him in the town, lying on his back in the park, singing to himself. Another time, he was found taking empty bottles from behind a café.

Then one morning as the sun came up, Moses ducked out of the dormitory building, along the small dirt road and down into town. He skipped over the main road and ventured out the other side of town. He poked around behind some of the shops and houses, but a dog started to bark, so he moved on. After the last house, there were a few shacks, and then some fields of maize stretched out before him. He wandered along and thought of the dried maize stalks that time he ran from the old white man's house. Maize all dried up and dusty like old sticks.

Past the fields was a small slow river. Its banks were choked with bushes and tall trees that grew high over the water. Some cows had been there to drink, and hoof prints and cowshit marked the dust. But now it was deserted.

Moses looked over his shoulder and walked down the river a little way before stopping and sitting down. He took off his shirt, then his pants and sandals. Finally he waded into the water, looking around to make sure he was alone.

He went under the water, feeling it pour over his entire head, and then hurried back up to the surface to check for other people. Once he was sure he was alone, he submerged himself again. The water was shallow and clear and he pushed his feet deep into the sand. He screamed under the water to hear the muffled noise it made, and then floated like a dead person until he was almost out of breath. He screamed underwater again and again until he was exhausted. Screaming all of the things he wanted to say to everyone, cursing all of the people he wanted to hate. He boxed, punched and fought an underwater war against even those who had helped him, but frustrated him: Kioso, Mama, George—all of them, together with Prosper.

When he got out, he sat on the bank and watched the flat river. On the other side, he could see how high the water had risen during the rains. He looked at a sausage tree dangling over the shallow water and the fat fruits that had fallen on the river bank. He watched the green pigeons on its branches. Moses had never seen a green pigeon before.

On the way back Moses sang Radi's songs. He walked the dust path back to town, but in his mind he was in Dar, walking the bright streets in the morning. Singing Radi and finding his way.

On Moses's return, he was reprimanded for disappearing, but the next week he went off again. Again, he swam in the river, and then he walked further, beyond the river and into the bush. He found some old cattle tracks and followed them. On the way back he saw other people, cattle-herders who nodded to him as they passed.

He returned, was reprimanded again, and the next week he went back again. Each time, it was different. Sometimes cattle were down at the river and young herders were bathing in the waters. At these times, Moses hid in the bushes and watched.

And each time, he ventured a bit further beyond the river. He made a game of it, trying to remember the exact spot he had turned around the last time, making sure he walked further the next time. Eventually, he would spend the entire day out wandering, and return to find George waiting for him in the coming darkness of evening.

During the week, Moses kept quiet, talked with Kioso, sat through classes without saying a word and played football. On Saturday or Sunday, however, he would disappear. Eventually, after George and his staff watched over him all weekend, he started going off during the week.

Then one day he took Kioso along, and the two splashed in the water and pretended they were back in Dar, swimming in the harbour. They mimicked the drunks and the prostitutes and the lepers with missing fingers. Kioso joined Moses the next week too, and then they were both reprimanded by George, who began to worry that their wanderings would influence the other students.

But there was no time for that. It was a Wednesday when they left in the dark of early morning. They reached the river in no time and did not even stop to swim, just kept walking. By midday, they reached a dried-up streambed. Moses had never walked so far before. He and Kioso celebrated by climbing the trees. Then they went on, following the cattle tracks that meandered between the acacias and termite mounds.

It got hot and they sat under a tree until it grew cooler, and then turned back. They continued on the cattle tracks, but never reached the river. The light began to fade, and Kioso said it was scary and reminded him of the time they jumped out of the lorry leaving Dar.

"No, it's not, Kioso. I've been out here a hundred times. Just keep walking."

Kioso pointed into the bush.

"But we never passed that tree before. I would have remembered it. Look at all those funny spikes on it."

"You just didn't see it before."

"I'm thirsty. I want to be back at school. It will be dinner soon."

"Let's just keep walking, Kioso. We just need to get out. First, we get out, then you can think about dinner, so walk faster." Moses spoke sternly, but he hadn't recognised the tree either. That river had better be ahead, he thought. And now all the cattle trails looked the same to him. In his body was the pang of fear that every lost person knows. The twitching in the chest, the panic, the questions in the mind, blurred by anxiety, about the merits of going forward and those of turning around. If he could just see beyond those trees ahead . . .

"Let's climb a tree."

"What?"

"That one. Come on."

"Why?"

"To see, Kioso. To see. Just to make sure we are going the right way," Moses lied.

The two boys climbed up a big acacia tree and looked out over the bush. But all they could see was a rolling landscape of low trees, all looking the same.

"I can't see anything!" Kioso wailed.

In the undulating terrain of hills and valleys, Moses could not see any landmarks or mountains in the distance, which he knew would have given him a sense of direction. In fact, he could not see anything of use in finding their way back. And darkness was falling quickly now.

Moses jumped down from the tree.

"We must have gone a longer way. No problem, Kioso. Let's just keep walking this way. Soon we'll meet some herd boy or something."

Kioso looked at Moses with a look of fear that Moses had seen before.

"Come on, Kioso," he said, more gently this time.

Very soon the light was only a deep blue disappearing fast around them. Moses stopped and sat on the ground. Kioso stood looking at him.

"What do we do?"

"Sleep here. *Sijui.* Nothing else to do."

Moses considered their situation—no food, no direction, night-time. *It will get cold out here, and there is no road in this place. And I have not seen any sign of a cow for a long time. What about wild animals?*

"I am sure we'll find some herd boy tomorrow coming through here. We just got to sleep here tonight. That's all."

"This is like last time."

And like the last time, Kioso and Moses curled under a tree, trying to shield themselves from the cool air. They had no fire or blanket or light. They thought of lions and the things of the wilderness. Of warm, safe places like the school or the ship hull or, for Moses, Mama's home or Grace's room. It was the continual paradox for him—running from stability, seeking freedom, but when trouble fell, dreaming of the comfort of a small charcoal fire and a bowl of beans behind Mama's shop. And as the night grew darker and the cool air got cold, the two huddled together for warmth in a shallow depression under some bushes.

In the morning they set out early, for they had not slept during the night, and the predawn hours had been sharp and cold. They continued on the path—what else to do?—but saw no signs of herders or cattle. Just winding paths that meandered through the trees. Occasionally they saw impala browsing in the woodlands. Sometimes a path would stop at a dried river bed or fade out into tall grass. At these times, they would turn around and walk back, to try and find another way. Nothing looked familiar. It was a new world and an empty place. They were just guessing now, as if walking in the dark with their hands stretched out in front of them.

Sometimes they would get demoralised and stop walking for a while. Kioso would cry and Moses would look at him and say nothing. His emotions were a mix of guilt at what he had led them into—again—and disdain for Kioso. As Moses would look in different directions for better paths, Kioso would sit on a stump and draw circles in the dirt. He looked, like always, to Moses for answers.

They were hungry. It had now been two days since they had eaten anything. The water they found in the dried river beds smelled like animal piss, but they drank it. And they kept moving, always walking. For Moses, sitting, doing nothing, felt worse than anything else. It confirmed how lost they really were, how distorted their sense of time and distance was. Moses somehow knew to look at the sun for guidance, but did not know what to do with what he saw.

The wilderness was a large and lonely place. It was not a place of giraffes and sunsets, like in the storybooks at the school. It was not a place for humans at all, Moses thought. It was long and hot and far from everything. The monotony of the landscape added to his feeling of desperation. There were no indicators, no street signs. The land was merely as it was—a flat dusty stretch of trees, which all looked the same.

Another night fell cold as the moon rose in a clear sky. Moses did not notice the brilliant stars above, or the rising of Jupiter. Beauty is irrelevant to those who are lost. The boys curled together again through the late hours of the night when the air got hollow and cold. But when morning came, the world soon turned hot, and they walked on. They moved more slowly this day, their energy low from hunger and fatigue. After only about an hour, they stopped to rest under a tree. Moses leaned against the tree with his hand over his forehead and Kioso lay down on the ground.

They had slept hungry for much of their lives, but this time their suffering was greater and they were weak.

Moses left Kioso and walked off to find something, anything to eat. He did not recognise the fruits of the bush, the edible plants. He did not know how to dig for tubers, how to eat grubs, or how to find wild honey. However, he saw monkeys eating a broken fruit from a baobab tree, and went to investigate. He had seen these fruits in the market in the city, and on some trees outside the towns. It was the first familiar thing he had seen in this wilderness, and he threw sticks into the branches until he dislodged the few remaining fruits, which he gathered in his shirt and took back to Kioso. The two ate and their hunger eased a little.

"Let's go." Kioso did not reply. He simply rose and followed Moses. He did not speak any more, and neither did Moses. They crossed a small swamp and stopped to drink. Then they walked into tall yellow grass that reached to their chests. The path began to fade under their feet as trails in the grass tend to do, until they were simply wading through grass, sightless and resigned. Just going forward, onwards into the abyss.

When the snake struck Kioso below the knee, he jumped back and fell and squealed like an infant. It was not the burning, electric sensation from the venom that made him jump, but the sight of the puff adder shifting and recoiling.

"Kioso! Get away from it." Moses yanked Kioso away from the snake, which moved under a bush. Kioso did not say anything, just held his leg and looked up at Moses. He did not scream from the understanding that the venom would take only a few hours to destroy his leg, then his body, then his life. No, he just held his leg and looked at Moses.

The two shuffled back out of the tall grass. They sat under a tree and looked at Kioso's leg, and the two fang marks deep in the skinny black leg of the boy. Moses was wide-eyed. He touched the skin on the leg. Kioso could feel the pain from the bite, stinging unlike anything he had felt before. Moses wiped some blood from the bite, but nothing more. What could he do? So they sat, scared, in the shade of a perfect acacia tree on the edge of the grasslands in the late afternoon.

Chapter 6

Much later they sat under a tree, looking at the place where the snake had bitten Kioso. They had given up walking not from being tired, or from the pain in Kioso's leg, or from any understanding of how snake venom worked. They stopped because they were just not getting anywhere.

Moses sat doing nothing, not able to fix a venomous bite on a kid with no chance. They didn't know much about snakes or any animals really, but they knew enough to understand that they had reached a point they had never been before. The view before them seemed different. They were not philosophical enough to wonder if this valley would be the last thing Kioso would see, or if the ground under this tree would be the last place he would visit, or if there would be any final moment of transition or clarity. They did not seek frantically for a solution, a way out, a cure, or a poultice to prolong Kioso's life. They could not run, and there was no place they could go that seemed better than where they now sat.

Kioso's leg swelled fast, reminding Moses of the bloated, dead-men legs of the homeless people back on the streets of Dar es Salaam. The leg bulged and took on odd shapes. The skin was tight and hard and its surface smooth, like the stomach bladder of a slaughtered goat.

The leg kept changing. Moses would look away at the valley, then at the land behind, then at Kioso's face. And when he looked back at the leg, a new bulge would have appeared under the skin, or a new kind of seeping stuff would be dripping down his leg like cooked fish fat. The leg took on not just a shape, but a life and evolution of its own. Both boys just sat back and watched it. Almost as if putting some distance between them and the leg would prevent it from jumping altogether on top of them.

The venom finally reached Kioso's brain. The formula of toxins designed for the simple destruction of a field-mouse had crept northwards, from leg to knee, up thigh and through the vast interior of his body to arrive in his head, his brain, and the sensations of his mind. Kioso would mumble, sweat, panic, grab Moses's arm, and then fall into a dreary sort of sleep that was not real sleep, but respite for a period of time from reality.

Death crawled into his bones. Or rather, gnawed its way there. Kioso did not know he was dying. He just knew he was scared, and did not have the strength to do anything. He looked up at Moses with eyes like those of a begging dog. Some drool slid from his mouth. He was thirsty, then had brief jolts of pain. Death took him as he gazed skyward into the thin canopy of acacia trees.

Had it been three days or four? Six? Moses tried to count the days by remembering where he had slept each night, what the place around him had looked like. Or how the sky had looked before he had slept. He knew there was that one cloudy night, and the one with the big tree above him, and the one when it had been so cold that he had never slept at all. He wandered, in his mind and with his legs. Sometimes when he looked out into the grasses, he saw him, the man. He was old, with a cane, and wearing a dark suit and a nice hat. Like a churchman, Moses thought. The image was peaceful. Moses would walk towards him, sometimes run to him shouting, but the man would get up slowly and walk away, and then Moses could not find him again. He would become frantic and angry. He also saw the churchman near some hills, sitting with his back to Moses on a fallen tree out in the sun in the middle of the day. Moses walked quickly to the tree, but again, the man was gone.

He saw brown parrots eating marula fruit. The ones that had fallen on the ground were full of insects, so he had to climb the tree and pick fresh ones. He carried some with him for later. He saw other fruits on a tree near a sandy river with no water, just a bed of sand and tracks and sticks, left behind from the rainy times. Some other birds, black-and-white ones, were eating these fruits. So he tried these too.

Lying down at midday to be out of the sun, he would dream. *The harbour, then I'll go to the road. Get food, walk. Sleep, back to the harbour, lie back in the old ship hull and look out at the water. And Prosper! I'll hit him again. In the grasses, I see people pulling fish nets, and I walk towards them, but they always disappear. They are hiding somewhere with the churchman.*

After some time, the sun no longer occurred to him. He would walk through the fierce heat of midday, exposed under the sun, and only after hours—how long?—would he wake from his spell and seek shade and rest.

Then he found strength again, without knowing that it was not from food—not real energy—but rather from the body entering the mode of survival. Any energy stored in his muscle, fat, organ or bone now fuelled his onward movement. His body allowed itself to be sucked, his flesh burned as the last source of fuel. Fruits gave energy, but not enough. Water was scarce, and only in a few mud holes, and then not for a long distance.

Then he found the eggs.

Eggs: a scavenger's gold. In the middle of a plain of dead grasses, there they were. Three beautiful eggs. Mottled brown, with an exquisite design no artist could create. Moses lifted one gently with his fingers and placed it in the cup of his other hand. He took it and the other two to the shade of a nearby tree and rested them gently back down on the earth. He chose one and cracked it on the tree, and it spilled out into his hand, most of it falling on the ground. Moses cursed and scrambled to slurp the yolk from his hand before it all slipped to the ground. He was furious at himself for wasting it. The next egg he held in his hand while he thought. He would not be stupid this time.

The simplest solution was the best, so he tilted his head back and cracked the egg into his mouth, filling it entirely, not a drop wasted. He swallowed it, and the next egg, then went back to the nest he had pilfered. He saw the sand grouse, francolin, plovers, larks, cisticolas all around him, but where were their eggs? He found none, and fell into despair again, head in his hands on the ground in the open sun next to the empty nest.

He searched harder. He decided to look over every patch of earth in that field for eggs. There must be more. On hands and knees, he looked under bushes, parting grasses, peering into scrapes in the dirt. He found another two, which he ate. Then, before the sun went down, he found another three. He slept that night, nauseated, under a tree near the field.

As soon as the sun rose the next morning, Moses went out into the grasses and began hunting again. He found no eggs that morning, but rested in the shade when the sun got hot, and searched again in the afternoon, finding two more eggs. He slept under the same tree again, sheltered on one side by a termite mound. The earth was soft, but as usual, it got cold at night. The next morning he set out again, and the morning after that. Then there were no more eggs. He spent another full day searching and found only grass, bushes, and flappet larks mocking him overhead.

Moses left his field and walked away.

Day, night, day again. He found water in a muddy patch, but hunger came back fiercely. The eggs were of the past, and there was nothing for him now but land. He walked as a soldier might, simply onwards, his body feeding off itself again.

Moses curled under trees for long periods of time, sometimes a whole day, sometimes awakening in fear and urgency to walk again. At other times, he would wake up and look up at the sky and the tree branches over his head and not think of anything. He started seeing the churchman again, and then never again, and he stopped thinking about him altogether. He would see other things, small things like soda bottle-tops, which ceased being soda bottle-tops when he went to pick them up. He would toss the flat bits of stone into the bushes or just let them fall from his hands. He did one time find a shred of plastic bag, which was real, and he carried it with him without questioning where it might have come from.

Moses and his strip of plastic reached the foothills of giant rocky outcrops emerging from the earth. They were hard granite, and Moses climbed the trail leading up and in between them through the *oleleshwa* trees that others might have known how to cut an arrow from, or a bow, or a firestick. But Moses knew nothing of bush-tools or plants, and when he reached the top of the peak, two eagles took flight, as if jumping from the cliff's edge. They dipped and flapped and picked up wind and rose and left him. Moses walked to the edge. Below him was an expanse, a distance vast from above, but narrow when on the flat ground below.

Moses had no intention of searching any more. He looked for no solution or direction. He did not squint to try and work out where he had come from, which trails he had followed, what his next move might be. He watched the eagles return and turn and disappear again. He watched flat thin clouds far away.

There were many small rodent-like creatures on the rocks. Like fat rats, Moses decided. They squealed at him. There were also many bottle-tops, which he spent time throwing into the emptiness below him. Nothing else seemed to be there, and he saw no animals out in the bush below. Just trees and grasses.

When Moses climbed down from the rocks, he curled under a tree and slept. He woke in the night, hearing noises, and was nervous, but then sat watching shapes and shadows cast by the moon passing above. By morning, he was asleep again, and he slept through the day, rising once to piss and stand in darkness looking at the rocky mountain. That night he did not dream of people, but rather of himself walking. He walked, searched, walked. There were no details in his dream. There were no elements of his past life at the harbour, at school, or even with Kioso. His dream was exactly like his life when he walked: a solitary existence wandering through the bush with hunger and thirst, and his only occasional emotion being one of failure.

Part 2

Chapter 7

The men sat laughing. They had stopped early to spend the afternoon resting and eating the last of the goat. The Maasai men in the group laughed and talked around a fire with tea and shade and company and goat meat. One of the men, Toroye, was not a Maasai, and sat to one side, a little outside the circle around the fire. Each time they stopped to make fire and tea, Toroye would sit with them, listening but not talking much, and then he would go to the side and lie down, on the ground, on his side with his arm bent under his head as a pillow. Sometimes, if the flies were bad, he would pull his shirt over his face to keep them and the light out. And if there was a nice smooth rock nearby, then he would lie on that instead of the ground, as long as it was in the shade.

Boyd took a small fold of greasy newspaper from the pocket of his shorts. Inside the paper was a square of plastic, torn from somewhere. He unfolded the plastic and took a pinch of tobacco powder between his thumb and forefinger, which he tucked up high between his upper lip and gum. He sucked and spat once, and leaned back against the tree. He flicked a few ants off his leg and listened to the men's chatter.

The days had been hard, hotter than normal, and hot early in the day too. He, Toroye, and the Maasai had set out early each day, walking, and at dusk they would stop, cook food, drink tea, and sleep. A few days earlier, they had bought a goat from a herder, and the men had taken it behind a tree where one of them had pinned down its limbs with his hands, while another pinned the head with his knee and then suffocated the squirming animal, its eyes bulging, until eventually there was no more than an occasional spasm. The men then sharpened their knives on the stones next to them, spread-eagled the carcass, gutted, skinned, and jointed it, and spread the pieces on the branches they had laid underneath. They paused to eat the warm kidneys, which they popped in their mouths like boiled eggs. One then returned from the bush with sapling branches, which he whittled into sharp stakes, green, fire-resistant, and flexible, for hanging the meat over the fire. To Boyd, this was a fair reward for the work and the long days on the hunt.

Now, a few days later, the goat was reduced to nothing more than the fatty smell it had left on the men. That and the head, which one of them had carried on the trail, and which now they put onto the fire. Often, when it seemed that the last piece of goat had finally been eaten, someone would fish out a limb or the testicles, or some other odd little bit. Boyd looked at the charred hair and blackened ears and white teeth, grimacing at him from the fire, and knew that he would never carry goat testicles in his pocket.

The sun fell that day behind the acacias, and the sunset was unremarkable over the flat country. The goat head, by now trimmed of its last edible bits, lay forgotten beside the fire, and the men were scattered on the ground, their *rubegas* wrapped around them, lost in a deep sleep. Boyd spat out what remained of the tobacco powder, took a swig of water, and got up. He stretched his arms behind his back and heard his sternum pop as it always did, then unbuckled his pack and took out a rolled-up *kongoni* hide, which he shook out and laid by the fire. He pulled out a blanket, took off his boots, and with his small pack for a pillow, he took a deep breath and rolled over to sleep.

The sun came up as it had gone down. Birds sang, but not much, and the day came about reluctantly and without brilliance. The country was grey and monotonous and flat, except for some soft rises on the horizon and a far-off mountain range to the north. It was dry and the land was parched, well into the final push of the dry season, holding on until the November rains. The grass was tough and woody, the earth pale, the dust deep and fine. The smaller waterholes had long since been reduced to hard wallows of dried mud, showing the tracks of the last to drink there. Only the few larger, deeper waterholes still had a little water. No rivers ran through this country.

Boyd and the men boiled tea in a *sufuria* and added a handful of maize powder to whiten it. They had run out of sugar several days earlier, and now carried only the essentials: tea, a *sufuria*, salt, some *ugali* flour, and the stale chapattis they had bought in the last village they had passed through days before. In his pack Boyd carried a five-litre water container, a drinking canteen, his blanket, and the dried *kongoni* hide for sleeping. They moved each day, and each day they set out not knowing where they would end up. They had left the truck some days before in a thick stand of *brevispica* brush by a waterhole they knew they could find again, when they had finished the hunt.

The sky was still grey when they drank the last of the tea and set off. The three Maasai went one way and Boyd and Toroye another. The Maasai were from a nearby village. Some days earlier, Boyd had passed through their village, and they had told him that they knew where the buffalo came to drink at night, and where they were resting during the day. Toroye had shaken his head, but stayed quiet. Boyd, against his better judgement, took the men along. It turned out as he had feared, and as Toroye knew it would: no buffalo, just thicker country and hungry men. So on the last morning, Boyd gave them each some shillings and a farewell, and he and Toroye were on their own again in the bush and in the quiet. They struck out along one of the big elephant trails leading west.

The trails were ancient highways blazed by generations of elephants connecting the scattered water sources that defined the landscape and gave it meaning. It was as if everything was designed with an emphasis on water and directions to it. On these trails, walking was easy, fast, and quiet, and this morning was no different. They had camped with the Maasai the night before between two waterholes. The last one they had checked showed no recent sign of buffalo, despite the insistence of the Maasai. At the next one they might see fresh tracks, rubs, but the country was hard going, and the distances long.

Peak dry season had left little food for game, and most buffalo had moved on to higher country and the well-watered river lands and mountains far away, the big herds with calves seeking the security of reliable water and good grass. But the old bulls stayed, alone, or with a few other bulls. You would not see them, only their signs: dung, tracks, a single black hair stuck in the bark of a *tortilis* tree. The bulls moved only in the witching hours of the night, when the wind dies and the world becomes quiet and the air, for a time, warm. That time of night when whatever had tried to stay awake, waiting, falls asleep. And then, an old buffalo would emerge to drink and wallow. He would take his hour and depart well before sunrise, with enough time to return deep into the bush, into the dense bowels of hookthorn thickets or the dark places of a deep *korongo* to wait out the day.

Here in the badlands, hunting was hard, and only for the purist. Old big bulls always seemed to choose the harshest and driest land, as if it offered some peace and quiet from the bustle of other game and movement and life—and hunters. Where a buffalo could live out his final days as a recluse. Here was a lonely place, and the only sense of community was among the birds.

The day got hot and the land pale. They followed the trail all morning through the *stuhlmannii* thorn, along a drainage with higher trees, into thicker bush, until they reached the small remnant of a waterhole. Three gardenia trees gave good shade, and under them it was finally cool. Boyd picked up a fruit from the ground and threw it. He looked for pythons in the trees, as they sometimes were, but gave up after a few minutes. He knew if he continued looking hard enough, he would find one, but didn't. Toroye walked to the edge of the shade to piss. Boyd sat on a gardenia root. The waterhole was dried mud, hard as if frozen. He looked down at the delicate antelope prints and the big potholes left by the elephants—and the old buffalo tracks. All old. "*Zamani*," he said to Toroye. "*Zamani sana*."

They carried on through the acacia, and the going got slow and thick. At last they punched through to the edge of a great expanse.

"Shit." Boyd rested his rifle, stock down, barrel up, against his waist. He took off his hat and put it back on again. It was noon and before them lay the floodplain, spreading far and treeless. They could just make out some trees on the horizon. Ahead lay only tall grass and thistles and distance. A game trail led out into the expanse. Boyd raised his binoculars to scan the plain, but then lowered them.

"Shit," he said again, and sat, pulling out his tobacco. Toroye whistled at the distance and took a few steps into it before coming back into the shade of the last tree. Boyd handed the tobacco to Toroye, who took a pinch and then also sat. "*Mbali sana*," he said, whistling again.

They didn't stop walking until they were halfway across the floodplain. They could see horizon trees to the east, west, south, and north. And in all directions, the trees in the distance shimmered with the heat. The game trail showed life from wetter times, the deep pits made by the feet of elephants that had passed months earlier, when the plain was a flooded marsh of black-cotton soil and green grass, a vastly different world from the thick grass and hard earth that it was now. Far out, they could see a lone hartebeest. Just a head and the shape of its horns bent out and up.

"God bless the hartebeest," Boyd said aloud, but to himself. "Out here, in the dry and nothing."

From four hundred metres away, the hartebeest watched them. Boyd raised his rifle and cradled his sights on it, breathed in once and out once to take aim, said "poof" and lowered the gun. He leaned it against his waist, pulled up his binoculars and looked at the hartebeest again. He lowered the binos, took off his hat, and wiped his forehead with his arm.

"*Tuwende*," Toroye said, and the two started to walk, Toroye's bow now crooked between his arms behind him, as he always carried it when the day got hot. Boyd knew a walk was long when Toroye stopped holding his bow in one hand, instead cradling it yoke-like behind his back, with his jacket, blotched black with grease and dirt, pulled back.

They carried on across the floodplain under the heat of the day. When a faint wisp of breeze could be felt, Boyd would lift his hat to let the air pass over the sweat on his head and cool him for a moment.

They didn't talk. It was a time and place for the mind to wander, for ground to be covered. It was still hot when they reached the first stand of tall *seyal* acacias lining the edge of the floodplain, where the soil changed from black to grey to red, where the land started to rise slightly, where vegetation other than grass began, where life continued once again.

They did not stop at the treeline but continued past it, as if they had still not put enough distance between themselves and the misery of the open country. They spooked a hare and kept walking, carrying on up into the brush, the gradual rise giving the land slight relief and elevation. They stopped under a gnarled *commiphora* tree. Toroye squatted and Boyd sat on the ground. Boyd scanned the country behind them with his binoculars, grimacing at the barren distance. Toroye pulled dried sap from the tree and chewed it.

"Let's find something to eat and a place to sleep."

They rose and walked further up to higher ground. They flushed some francolin and marked where they landed. Boyd then stood still while Toroye took from his quiver a bird arrow with no metal head, only a wooden shaft whittled to a fine point. He crossed one leg over the other, planted firmly, his body leaning forward, head straight, posture strong. He then snap-fired in one fluid movement, and the arrow struck home and the bird became a frenzy of flapping feathers.

The impaled bird tried to run with the metre-long arrow through its body, but could only flap wildly and run in one direction. Boyd watched the bird twist in circles and thought that when he was younger, he would have found the sight funny. Toroye snatched the bird, removed the arrow, wrung its neck, squatted, and pulled a thin firestick from his quiver. He broke off a piece of dead wood from a fallen branch, laid it flat, placed the end of the firestick on it, and began spinning. He stopped, spat into his hands, and continued spinning. Soon there was smoke from the friction and then small ashy coals, which he placed in a fistful of dried grasses. He then waved the grasses in his hands, passing the air through them, until he had created a small flame. He placed this small fire on the ground, added more grass and sticks, then placed the splayed bird on the fire.

The heat ended when the sun set. The one reliable thing. He and Toroye sat on the bedskin around the fire, silent, feeling no obligation to make small talk.

Toroye was a hunter-gatherer whose people lived in the bush in small nomadic communities, moving with the seasons, moving with game, and living at other times in small, dismal villages of the bush. His people were largely dispersed and overrun by the aggressive and powerful cattle people of the area. But in the remote wilderness, they endured. Avoiding conflict, collecting honey. Life was hard, but unlike almost all other peoples, they had never experienced famine. They lived off the land, and even in the driest times, the land always provided just enough to survive. Scorned by many as outcasts, as poor and worthless, they were people whose inclination was simply different, whose culture was not bound by the structures of pastoral life, the rules, the hierarchy, the societal demands. Rather, they were free—turning their eyes to the wilderness as a place to live, a place that was home.

Boyd had known Toroye for many years through hunting in the area, and always sought him out to join him on hunts. Sometimes, coming into the area, he would find him easily, deep in the recesses of some shady drinking-place, inebriated and alone in the silence. Other times, Toroye would be gone, somewhere off in the bush, living off what he shot and what he found. In the past, he would have worn hides and skins. Now he wore cut-off pants, a ragged shirt and jacket, all stained with blood, sweat, fat, and ash. But his craft remained the same, and the bush was still his home.

"And tomorrow?" Toroye asked.

Boyd shrugged.

"Just carry on," Toroye suggested fatalistically. Boyd chuckled to himself. That's about right, he thought.

"There." Toroye pointed north with the twig he had been using to pick his teeth. "Water there. Must be."

There was no noise in the night. Boyd hated camping in a silent place. It made him feel that there was no game around. And here it was true. They were in a stretch of bush where all things traverse, and none remain.

When morning came, they did not bother with fire or tea, but left the place quickly, leaving only the cold coals of the previous night's fire behind them.

The early morning was cold and they walked fast for two hours to make ground. When it started to warm up, Boyd shed his jacket, stopping to put it in his pack. A lone hyena observed them from a distance, facing them head-on. Toroye and Boyd looked back, all three of them assessing each other in silence. Boyd lost interest and pulled the tea out of his pack, and Toroye made fire and boiled water. The hyena backed off a little, then stood broadside and watched them again. When they packed their things and rose to leave, the hyena loped off into the bushes and disappeared.

Another stand of *stuhlmannii* thorn, another *mbuga*, another endless plain. The cool morning sky left them, and the sun returned overhead. The ground was now parched and white, with a crusty surface like snow. They found some giraffe bones, ancient, white, cracked, and scattered. The white bones on the white ground made Boyd wonder what the scene had looked like when the animal had died. Maybe it had been green.

The hyena appeared again. Boyd lifted his binos and looked at it. It was the same hyena as before—old, alone, one ear chewed off. Worn teeth, maybe some infected wound. As they walked through the morning on the white plain, the hyena trailed them. When they stopped, it stopped. When they rose to walk on, it followed. Eventually it disappeared from view.

Boyd carried a .470 double-barrel rifle. New, it would have been an expensive gun, well beyond his means. But he had bought it secondhand from a Portuguese professional hunter. The man said he was selling all his belongings to start a new life. He said he was moving back to Lisbon to open a restaurant. Carved into the stock were the initials M.A.R. for Manuel Antonio . . . something. Boyd had forgotten the last name.

The man who sold it to him said it had belonged to a friend of his who had been killed by a buffalo. He had shot it twice, but the buffalo had kept on charging, crushing the man into the ground, pushing his broken body deeper into the mud and thrashing from side to side to stab him with its horns. At the time, he had wondered if it was a bad omen, but he bought the gun anyway.

When they saw the hyena next, it lay dead as a stone out in the open plain ahead of them. It lay on its back, its legs spread like a dog wanting its belly rubbed. Toroye poked it with his bow. Boyd touched its eye with the barrel of his rifle. Two men standing over a dead hyena in a dry plain far from anything. The hyena's teeth were bared in an eerie grimace. The animal was old, but uninjured. No wounds, no reason—it had just up and died. Toroye leaned on his bow to rest his legs and looked at it without expression.

They carried on, leaving the hyena where it lay. No vultures circled. Soon its belly would swell, ballooning with the trapped gases. There didn't seem much to scavenge it here, nothing to break into the carcass, no vulture to eat into its eye sockets and anus, no jackal to tug at its belly and pull at its entrails. Eventually, it would be a dried-out piece of skin, a taut canvas over a frame of bones, its meat hard-cured leather. Insects would get to it at some point. Botfly, ants. Perhaps only ants. A lonely death.

The men passed through a woodland and descended into a slight valley, where there were signs of game. It was more of a depression than a true valley, but it held seepage and underground water and greener vegetation. A dried river bed ran along through it, filled with old tracks. Boyd and Toroye sat in the shade of a large sausage tree, its heavy fruits hanging above them. They sat, sucked on tobacco, rested, both thinking of the next move. Under the tree were tracks from a lone kudu, which they knew had come to eat the flowers of the sausage tree. Toroye picked one up, twirled it by its stem, and let it fall.

Boyd rested his elbows on his knees and looked through his binos. He scanned the treeline on the other side of the valley. He lowered the binos slightly, looked, and then lifted the binos to look through them again. Toroye also looked into the distance, at the low lump under a tree in the shade that Boyd had spotted. It looked like an animal sleeping in the shade. Like a lion escaping midday heat, but much smaller. Just a dark bump. It reminded Boyd for a moment of the hyena.

"*Tuwende kuangalia*," Toroye said, and they rose to investigate. They approached slowly out of habit. They stopped every few moments to look through the binos again. After the third pause, Boyd jerked his head back from the binos. He looked again quickly, then handed the binos to Toroye. All they could make out was a shirt and an arm visible through the branches. When they approached, Moses was motionless.

Chapter 8

In sleep, lost and far, Moses walked on a flat plain looking for eggs. In his dream, he knew he had already searched for days without finding any. As he crawled on all fours to peer inside a big bush, he felt the branches scraping and knocking against his legs as he crawled further and further into the bush. Inside it was dark and he could not see, only feel. He groped the earth, in branches, always thinking of snakes, but needing eggs.

When Moses woke, Toroye was poking him with his bow. When he saw the two figures above him and Boyd's large-brimmed hat silhouetted against the sky, he scrambled to his knees.

"Whoa! *Hakuna wasiwasi.* Don't worry. Easy, child." Toroye crouched down to Moses's level and reached his hand out to the boy. Moses slumped back to the ground.

Boyd pulled off his pack and handed the water canteen to Toroye, who opened it and handed it to Moses. Moses drank and wiped his nose. After some time, Moses was able to tell the men his story, and they pulled out a stale chapatti, and he ate.

Boyd looked out into the wilderness, then to the sky as a farmer might do when trying to judge the weather. He took off his hat, hung it on a branch, and walked into the sun to piss. Toroye came and stood next to him. He gave Boyd a look that said "Now what?", and Boyd shrugged. "I guess that's it. *Lazima kurudi sasa.*"

It should have been easy. Moses now had food and water. Toroye knew the quickest way back to the truck. They could do it in three hard days' walking and two nights, depending on how Moses's strength held.

Boyd squatted and lifted Moses over his shoulder, and carried him on his back. Moses bobbed up and down, looking at the man's strange reddened and hairy skin and his big arm carrying the gun. He could see the different colours of the wood on the rifle stock, the grains of the original tree, and the stains from miles of sweat darkening the grip of the stock to almost black. He could feel the man's sweat and could see the salt of it in white-crusted stains at his collar.

Moses's mind was still in a haze. He did not even feel elation at his rescue. He just watched Boyd's gun and Toroye's legs and feet. He noticed the scratches on them, and the faded grey of the tyre-rubber of his sandal straps. Toroye's gait was practical, not graceful. He walked in hard, choppy steps, pounding the earth as he went. This was his stride for covering ground. When he hunted, however, the entire demeanour of his body would change. His crouch would lower, his steps soften.

When they paused to rest, Boyd would lower Moses. And when they started walking again, Boyd would lift the boy back onto his shoulders. Nobody spoke. They trekked on into thicker woodlands of acacia and *commiphora*. The beauty of the flat-topped trees and golden grass went unnoticed. At dusk, they stopped to camp.

The fire was bright that night. Toroye started fire under a thick log and added heavy branches. In the cool air, the heat was welcome. Boyd spread out the *kongoni* hide, laid Moses on it next to the fire, and rested the boy's head on the pack. He handed Moses the canteen. "Listen, child. You need to drink water—a lot." Moses drank and ate more, slowly, and at first it made him feel nauseated, but he continued.

Moses slept deeply that night, warm, belly-full, snug under a blanket and between two men whom he did not fear.

In the morning they set out, trekking uneventfully for most of the day. Baobab trees and their fruits were scarce in this country. They needed food. When they came across a lone male impala, Toroye motioned them to stop and Boyd lowered Moses to the ground behind a termite mound. He wiped the sweat off his hands, took off his hat and loaded two shells into the rifle. They could have saved shells by having Toroye shoot the animal with an arrow, and his .470 was far too heavy a calibre for an impala—but something made Boyd want to kill the animal. Frustration, or maybe a simple bloodlust that had never gone away. They needed meat, so at least he had a good reason, if he cared to have one.

The wind was good and into his nose as he stalked the antelope. Terrain was good too, and he approached noiselessly. He had cover from some termite mounds as he crept up, rested his rifle on a fallen branch, and relaxed his back and neck. The impala was close and standing broadside. Boyd cradled the sights, aimed behind the shoulder, and squeezed the trigger.

The gun's report was immense and louder than anything Moses had heard since leaving the orphanage. The impala fell in its place. No running. It wheezed, coughed up chunks of lung and bloodclot, and kicked once or twice. By the time Boyd approached it, life had already seeped from its eyes in a way that, despite the necessity of the hunt, made him feel remorse. The calibre of the bullet, designed to stop an elephant or buffalo, had made a violent wound in the animal, its front left shoulder dangling, broken and at an odd angle. Boyd lifted its leg and then laid it back to the ground. He cradled the antelope's soft muzzle in his hand as one would hold a loved dog.

Toroye approached and slit the impala's throat without ceremony. He and Boyd then set about field-dressing the carcass as Moses looked on. He watched them cut it up the middle and saw Toroye reach inside, take hold of the trachea, and heave out the mass of organs in one long pull, taking care not to puncture the stomach. He and Boyd then turned the impala on its side to empty the gathered blood. They butchered the carcass crudely, slicing tendons, cracking joints, separating legs, extracting the backstrap. Toroye then made a fire while Moses helped Boyd hang the body parts from a tree to be loaded into plastic bags and carried the next morning. Toroye roasted the liver and kidneys and heart on a skewer and laid some meat over the flames.

It was almost evening by the time they had all eaten, but as they settled down for the night, they heard gunfire in the distance. Several rapid, chaotic shots. *Rap. Rap rap. Rap, rap, rap. Rap.* Toroye and Boyd looked at each other and then in the direction of the shots, and listened for more. Perhaps it was another hunting party with a vehicle that could drive them out.

Hoping to find the other hunters before it became fully dark, they jumped up and walked quickly into the thick brush in the direction of the shots. Game trails wound narrowly through the thick *stuhlmannii*, and the land got flatter and the bush thicker. They walked for some time. At last they heard voices ahead and saw flashlights. They carried on through the thick tangle of brush to find the people.

When they emerged into the small clearing, they came upon the dead elephant. Poachers were hacking at the giant carcass, which lay on its side in a dark pool of blood. If they had been able to view the scene without surprising the men, they would have seen the pangas, axes, and saws at work extracting the ivory, the men standing high up on the carcass with flashlights, the others smoking nearby, the automatic rifles leaning against trees. They would have noticed men's feet covered in blood, their arms painted with it, and shards of flesh sprayed upwards and into the men's hair by the chopping and cutting and tugging.

The elephant lay violated on the earth amongst the men. Bloodied handprints lay on its skin like ancient rock paintings. Two large men in hats, one wearing a beret and the other a floppy hat full of holes, stood to the side directing the men. Most of the others wore rags, sarongs, and sandals.

If Moses had had time to observe, then the size of the beast would have been truly evident and the violence of the butchery clearer as well. He would have seen the trunk in a paste of blood and mud unfurled and flat and stepped over and on by the poachers.

If Moses could have watched the scene unnoticed, he would have been amazed at the length of the tusks, the whiteness of the fat around their roots, and the deep, wide cavities left in their places. He would have seen the men stuffing grass inside the tusks, and departing with them, leaving the rest of the beast to the silence of the circle of trees.

But when they emerged into the clearing, there was no time for observation. They came into the poachers' private scene, and the startled men reacted with panic. When the men saw Boyd and his rifle, they lunged for their AK-47s, chambering rounds and firing wildly. Chaos erupted.

Moses heard bullets passing by his head and the snapping of branches and shattering of tree bark. He would later struggle to understand how, in the frenzy of the scene, he would be able to remember the feeling of wind, the breeze of the flying bullets. Boyd yanked him back behind his body, shielding Moses from the gunfire. And the shower of bullets continued.

It was perhaps two, three times that Boyd was hit, or maybe more, and he cursed and held his stomach and continued pulling Moses behind him and down.

"Go there!" Boyd pointed into the darkness, and Toroye grabbed Moses by the arm, and they ran and dove into the brush on their bellies.

Boyd crouched behind a fallen tree. The poachers took cover at the end of the clearing, frantic and shouting and rattling off their guns.

When Moses heard the first deafening report of Boyd's .470, he pressed his face harder into the ground. He looked up to see a poacher with his left shoulder blown off. Toroye snapped off a couple of arrows, struck one man, and the AK-47s rattled back at them, sending him and Moses back to the ground. Among the clatter of machine-gun fire, Moses heard Boyd fire twice more, then pause, then fire twice again. Aside from the man with no shoulder or arm, two others lay dead. Another knelt screaming, cradling his entrails in his hands.

A scatter of bullets swept over where Boyd was hiding, and he cried out again. Moses saw him scramble for better cover behind the elephant carcass. Toroye continued to shoot arrows. Beams from dropped flashlights shone along the ground. In the fragmented light, Moses could see Boyd, crouched in the pools of elephant blood, dark and shiny. The sound of the gunfire was almost drowned out by the shrieking of the wounded man. Trapped in the crossfire, he knelt trying to gather his intestines until he caught another bullet in the arm, then another that sent him to the ground.

Before Moses could hear Boyd fire again, he and Toroye were sprayed by machine-gun fire. Toroye jerked him away by his arm, forcefully and fast and into the darkness of the bush. The noise went on, the clatter of machine-guns and the booming of the .470, the cries and the shouting. Moses and Toroye stopped to look back just long enough to make out the shapes and shadows of the poachers now converging on Boyd and the giant dark heap of the elephant. Boyd was hunched over, clutching himself. One of the men shouted above the rest, and a shot was fired and then another. Boyd dropped to a knee and slumped to the ground. Toroye pulled Moses away and into the bush.

The man in the beret wiped Boyd's gun clean. If there were any bullets remaining in Boyd's gun, he would have taken them as well, but there were none.

Toroye pulled Moses onto his shoulders and ran. They passed for a long time through a wide thicket of low acacia. Every few minutes, Toroye would stop, tilt his head to listen, and then carry on walking fast. Once they heard snapping branches and once Moses thought he heard a voice.

After some time, they exited the acacia, and Moses could hear the soil beneath Toroye's feet change from fine dirt into coarser earth with small stones. He could feel the gradient change, as they rose out of the depression of thickets. Moses no longer had a sense of time to determine how long they had walked. His mind wandered as he recalled Boyd shielding him from the bullets.

Night was full now and darkness complete. There was no moon and an overcast sky blocked out the stars. They knew men were chasing them, and they moved quickly through the darkness on game trails that Toroye followed not by sight, but rather by touch and rhythm. He navigated the trails blindly, his feet guided by the terrain, as if they were floating on a river, taken by the current, their course determined by rocks, eddies, sand bars, bends in the winding path of water. Toroye's eyes sought not landmarks, distance, or details, but were turned inwards, into the centre of his mind. His body moved where he felt it pulled.

Deep into the night, Toroye finally slowed. He came to a halt, and then, with delicate movements, he picked his way through the brush, moving each branch from in front of them. He clambered over rocks, and Moses felt cooler air. They had arrived at a cave. At the entrance, Toroye lowered Moses. He coughed to alert any leopard possibly hiding in the cave, and then snipped leafy branches from the bushes by the entrance. Moses then felt Toroye's hand on his head pushing it lower, telling him to crouch down, as they entered the hollow of cold darkness.

The floor of the cave was cold sand. Toroye spread the branches he had cut to make a bed for Moses. The two then lay down, Moses on his bed and Toroye next to him in the sand. It was cold, but Moses's head was resting on branches of wild sage, their soft leaves cushioning his head and comforting his body and mind so that he could finally fall asleep.

In the weak blue light before dawn, Moses woke and saw Toroye sitting at the cave's entrance. Moses rose and sat next to him, and looked down into the world below them. Nothing moved. The earth was like a giant reptile waiting for the sun's heat to give it enough energy to begin the day.

"I know where we are," Toroye told him, pointing to scattered bones and ashes near the cave's entrance. "From Ndorobo people," he said. "I am Ndorobo." Moses looked at the bones of what had been a small antelope, and the place where it had been cooked some time earlier.

"How are you feeling?" Toroye asked. Moses nodded. Toroye threw a bone down into the bushes. A scrub robin shrieked out a call, the sound of buzzing flies began, a pair of doves took off from a bush, and the light arrived suddenly, as it does on some days in the wilderness. The two rose and descended to flat ground.

They walked waist-deep through the yellow grasses that feathered their sides with their arrowhead tips, discarding ticks and seeds. With their movement, they pushed into a wave of silence and concealment. Whenever they stopped, however, to eat sap gathered in the elbows of the *commiphora* trees, to stand under their thin shade, to watch and listen, to feel and to not move, the world would come into its rhythm, embracing them. They had become invisible to it, for they had become part of it, able now to see it from the inside out. The land had accepted them, and now it concealed them.

They walked quickly all morning. They stopped for a brief rest under a tree, thirsty but with no water. Then Moses heard it. Something different, like someone knocking on a door. It stopped and then started again, and Toroye turned to Moses. "Ndorobo," he said motioning with his chin in the direction of the sound. "Let's go."

The man did not see them, but the woman did. The man was halfway up a tree, standing on a wide limb, slamming his honey axe into the side of the tree, not concerned about his surroundings, or the approach of Toroye and Moses. The woman stood below him.

At first Moses did not know what to think of the man and woman. They looked like the poor, homeless drunks at the harbour, those ones who scavenged through the rubbish bins along the harbour road. They wore rags and had rough hair with grass stuck in it, and bits of cloth wrapped loosely around their waists.

Toroye walked towards them, speaking in a language that Moses had never heard before. The woman responded without surprise, as if people appeared from the bush all the time. And for them, this was indeed normal, since they and other Ndorobo roamed the wilderness gathering and hunting, and seeing each other from time to time.

The man in the tree stopped chopping and leaned against a branch to look down at them. Toroye sat down next to where the woman was standing as they continued talking. She handed Toroye some water and food, a bit of meat.

"Come here." Toroye motioned to Moses. "Eat this. They are Ndorobo. I know them. Come, drink water, eat. We'll go with them."

The man waved smoke from a smouldering stick with one hand, and chopped into a beehive in the side of the tree with the other. The bees swarmed, dispersed by the smoke. The man reached into the hole, all the way to his shoulder, so far that the side of his face was pressed against the tree. He pulled out heavy chunks of honeycomb, dripping with honey and pollen, and passed them down to the woman.

The woman took a large piece of comb full of succulent bee larvae and stuffed it in her mouth. She ate it, then another as large, and another, and handed some to Toroye, who devoured large chunks, the honey dripping down onto the few wiry hairs on his chin. He handed a piece to Moses.

Moses looked at the comb, licked the honey and ate it savagely. He paused to break off another piece, and only then realised he was eating the larvae. He picked up one of the white maggots, held it out and looked at Toroye for confirmation. Toroye just motioned for him to eat, and Moses did.

He continued to eat until he felt sick, like the time he had been lost before, when he had eaten the leaves. He drank the water they gave him, managed not to vomit, and slowly started to feel better.

The man descended from the tree and they all moved to another place some distance from the hive. The men and woman ate most of the hive, incredible portions of honey and larvae, and the man then lay back under a tree and looked at the boy properly for the first time. Toroye told them the story of the poachers, and the man turned to Toroye, speaking seriously and pointing a stick in one direction.

Chapter 9

Moses spent his twelfth birthday on the floor of a temporary grass structure. It was more of a shelter made of gathered sticks, mud, and grass than a proper hut. And he woke up on his twelfth birthday thinking about Boyd. He thought of being carried, and of Boyd's eyes and his hat and his gun. To Moses, Boyd was a mysterious thing, a person he had known only for a flash of time, but one who had saved him.

Moses sat up. He then thought of Kioso, but quickly put him out of his head. The thought of Kioso meant returning to nothing of value, for he saw no value in his life as it had been, or as it now was. Boyd was a mystery; Kioso was sadness.

He had stayed with Toroye and the Ndorobo couple for several weeks. He rarely left the hut of twigs and grass. He was ill. He had a problem with his stomach, and everywhere else in his body, it seemed. The Ndorobo had a name for what he had, but he forgot it. Mainly he was tired. But for the first time he had no anxiety, and the tension that he had held in his chest for so long was gone. He was just tired.

He spent a lot of time with the woman. He would walk with her near the huts and dig up tubers and other edible things from the ground. Some of these things she would peel and boil for a long time, and make him drink for his stomach. Others they would eat right out of the earth. Sometimes they went to the big baobab trees to gather the fruits, the same kind he remembered eating when he was lost. They would throw sticks up into the branches to dislodge the fruit, which they would collect and bring back to camp. The woman also had a series of pegs sticking out of some of the trees, like a ladder, which she would climb up to look for honey hives.

Toroye and the man hunted often. The man had a long bow and arrows like Toroye, and a quiver made of hard leather. On his bow were thick bands of eland hide and baboon fur, which Moses liked and actually thought were beautiful. He admired the bow's polish, worn from the sweat of the hands that carried it, and from use and ability. It bent in a perfect arc. Initially, the bowstring was too tight for Moses to draw fully, but the man adjusted the tension and taught Moses to use it near the huts, until eventually Moses was able to hit tree-trunks at some distance. The man would always laugh when Moses's shot was true.

Toroye and the man returned from their hunts sometimes with meat or honey, and sometimes with nothing at all. Once they returned with a lesser kudu. It had an almost bluish coat with stripes, white tear marks on its face, and a high spiral of horns. It was immense, and Toroye brought Moses over and gave him the knife and showed him how to cut out pieces.

But mainly Moses stayed in the hut or near it. He watched the man and woman, what they did, and how she worked. He saw them laugh, and the man would tell stories that would make Toroye giggle, with a child's laugh. The man talked often. Around the fire each night, the man would tell long stories, with whistles and arms flailing about, and he would sometimes get up and re-enact scenes. Even Moses would laugh sometimes, in spite of not understanding the Ndorobo words.

But in the background of his thoughts, there always remained the horror of what had happened to Boyd, the violence of his death. There was something about the quantities of blood that haunted him. The wetness of blood on the earth. The speed of events. And the panic and his face pressed to the ground as he lay on his belly to escape the bullets. Then Boyd pulling him by the arm to shelter him from the bullets.

As time went on, however, his thoughts evolved from details into questions. Boyd had saved him—a person had actually died for him.

And he thought: Why would he do that?

At times, other Ndorobo men would show up at their camp, and one time, another man and woman. When visitors arrived, the couple would share their food, and everyone would eat. Some stayed a few days, eating their food and sleeping at their fire before moving on, disappearing one morning. And one day, the man and woman told Moses they were moving. Seasons were changing. Rains were coming and it was time to move to another part of the valley. One day they lived in huts, the next day they moved, carrying all that they had, which was little. Moses and Toroye went with them.

At a new location, they built small shelters like the last ones, and Moses again spent a lot of his time inside sleeping. The quick steps that had enabled him to survive at the harbour, and which had brought him to this place, were gone. He was, for the first time in his life, slow.

Moses would watch the woman from his resting place inside the hut. He could see her through the opening of the hut, making flour from baobab fruits, cooking and storing things, doing chores like preparing hides, getting water, tending the fire. He would look at her hair, which was short and uncared for and grey in places, not from age, but from dust and ash. Aside from crazy women on the streets, Moses had never seen a woman with such messy hair. In his experience, a woman's hair was always a tidy thing, except in the mornings or those times when women were in the beauty salons getting their hair fixed up and made pretty. Or when women would sit on beer crates or stools outside the shops and braid each other's hair.

Moses thought of Grace and the few nights he had spent in her small room, and of her frizzled hair when she woke up in the morning. He remembered eating tripe soup with her. He was glad he had never stolen anything from her room. She was just a regular young woman when she took off all the prostitute clothes and make-up. Moses thought of the picture in her room, of the family near some farm. Maybe she was just like him, with a father from a farm where people worked in fields and everyone stayed together. And she went to the city to make money. She had a room, yes, but not a whole lot of things—just some clothes, a bed, a cooker, what else? Spending her time standing on street corners. Having to give sex to men. She had more money than he ever did, though. More money than Toroye and the man and the woman. They didn't have any money. Nowhere and nothing to spend it on out here.

In fact, they were sort of like him. No home—just a pile of sticks—no job, no money. Moving around from place to place, going where the getting was good and life a bit easier. Like him, he thought, just surviving. But not like him, he also thought. Not at all. Somehow, moving around, finding food, surviving in this place—for them, it made sense, it seemed right. They belonged here. He watched the woman sitting under the shade of a tree pounding the fruits into flour, singing a song to herself he couldn't understand. He looked at her and saw that she was happy. He realised that she did not look like she wanted to be somewhere else. In Dar, everyone looked like they wanted to be somewhere else.

Moses lay on his side to rest. He continued to watch the woman until he fell asleep, and when he dreamed, he dreamed of Grace.

They walked out of her room to go and eat. Then he left her and walked to Mama Tesha's house to ask about Kioso. He roamed the streets like always, and saw hundreds of young men slouched against a wall. A truck passed by, dragging an exhaust pipe, and the crowd turned to listen to it grating along the road. The driver seemed not to notice or care. The line of youths stretched further than Moses could see. Moses could see their mouths moving, in a constant murmur of unintelligible nonsense like the droning of a boat engine. Then all he could see were their mouths, and they were silent, just hundreds of lips moving up and down like gaping fish mouths. What were they waiting for?

He walked on down the line to where a man sat at a desk with papers. He stamped things and the men waited. The man at the desk wrote things slowly. Moses could see the letters, each one written, a big "S" or "D" in dark ink. The man was short but large and sweating, and had a fishbone sticking out from his pocket. Some of the men in the line were impatient, others held their hands over their heads to block out the sun. Some had blank expressions, as if not wanting to see the line stretching before them, or the slowness of the man at the desk. They all stood there trying for something, but knowing that there was probably no point.

Moses knocked at Mama Tesha's door and she told him that the police had called her and that they had found Kioso. She led Moses inside by the arm and sat him down and told him that Kioso was dead, that the white man had killed him. She gave Moses a soda with a straw, and he held it, but did not drink. He wanted to know more, but she didn't tell him anything else, just looked at him with her eyebrows tucked in. She stood up and over him and looked down on him as if to say "You are no good and worthless."

"Come drink," said the woman as she crouched at the entrance of the hut. She held a chipped tin cup towards him filled with hot dark red fluid.

"Drink." She motioned with her hands. Moses sat up and took the cup and blew at the steam and took a small sip. The woman left and tended the fire. Moses thought back to his dream as he drank.

When Moses stepped outside the hut, he vomited, and the woman approved. The drink was good for him, she told him. She said he should not drink water now, but rather sit next to her in the shade. She did not smile much, but her forehead was full of expression. When she spoke or sang, six or seven lines on her forehead wrinkled together. Although the woman spoke some Swahili, she preferred to speak to Moses in her language, even though Moses could not understand the words.

She touched Moses. At times when he lay down, he would feel her touch his head, his hand. One time he woke to find her rubbing the top of his hand. When he opened his eyes, she continued looking at him and rubbing his hand. When she gave him a drink or food, she often touched him when handing it to him. At first, Moses found it was strange, foreign even, the gentle touch. But after a while, it became normal, and he did not notice it any more.

Toroye and the man came back that day with no food. They had hunted hard and long, spending the night out in the bush. When they walked back into camp silently at midday, Moses stood up. He watched them lay their bows against a tree, sit without speaking, and then take food handed to them by the woman. Moses wanted to ask about the hunt and why they had not gotten anything, but knew better.

The men ate and then slept. Moses thought about the day when he and Toroye had first encountered the couple collecting honey. They had now stayed with them for some time, and the couple never seemed to ask why or for how long they intended staying. He and Toroye ate their food, slept in their huts, accepted their nurturing. They gave, but asked for nothing in return. Other Ndorobo would arrive from time to time, and would also eat and sleep and leave with little spoken thanks. Everything seemed to belong to everyone here, for people owned what the land could give them, and the land belonged to everyone. Or was it that nothing belonged to anybody? But they *had* nothing, in a place where there were no *things*, just land and sky and fruits and animals. Water and trees and rocks and caves in which to sleep out of the wind and rain.

The next day Toroye and the man left early and returned early too, with an antelope as small as a small dog. After they brought it back and skinned and jointed it, Moses picked up the head, a tiny thing, and cupped it in his hands. Its eyes were very large and its nose was strange and tube-like. To Moses, the nose looked like those of the fish he had seen in the market by the harbour. Moses held up the head by its tiny horns so its petite face looked back at him. He went behind the huts and into the low brush and buried it. He did not know why. The hole was deep and good, not like the scrape he had made when he had tried to bury Kioso, and he took care when he pushed soil back over it. Handful by handful, he sprinkled earth over the head, covering the grave.

When he returned to the fire where Toroye and the man and woman were cooking the meat, they took him by the arm, made him sit and eat, and then laughed and told him that they had never seen anyone bury a dik-dik head before. "That's food to eat, not bury in the ground!" Toroye laughed his childlike giggle, and passed a small antelope leg to Moses to eat.

That night he fell asleep in the hut, listening to Toroye breathe deep and loud beside him. It was a warm night, with a soft breeze coming through the twigs of their hut. When he stepped outside in the night to piss, he looked at the stars and the half moon overhead, visible through the clouds passing beneath them.

✿

After some days, Toroye said Moses was not ill any more and that it was time to leave. Time to take Moses back to where he came from. Toroye packed some meat, and told Moses they would walk for a couple days to a small village, and from there they would find a truck, and the truck could take Moses back to Bangata.

Moses thanked the man and the woman, and the woman touched his head and turned and went back to her work. And Toroye and Moses walked out of camp.

Moses went silently but sadly. He did not protest, and it did not occur to him to do so, but as he walked away through the bush, he felt as if he was being evicted, hurried away. He still had things he needed to say, to complete. It was all too sudden for him. Why did he have to leave?

But he followed Toroye obediently, redirecting his emotions back inside, as he had done so many times in the past in order to survive. *Kioso, Boyd—they are dead people. Toroye and these people—they don't want me and soon they will be gone too. It's just me, and that's how it is.*

After two nights and a day they arrived in a small village, where they found an old truck driven by a Maasai man. The truck bed was full of Maasai, goats, and sacks of maize-meal. Toroye talked to the driver and gave him money, which Boyd had previously paid him. Moses climbed into the truck bed. He told the driver not to let the boy off until he reached Bangata. After that, Moses would return to the school on his own.

Toroye turned to Moses and put his hand on his head. "*Nenda salama,* child." Moses did not respond. He had nothing he could say, so he sat on a bag of maize-meal as the truck started down the road, and waved at Toroye, who turned and walked back into the bush.

The truck bounced, spat, coughed, and sent dust over and onto the passengers in the back. The journey reminded Moses of the time with Kioso in the big lorry, when they jumped out and met the old white man. The Maasai man who owned the goats chatted to Moses about his family, asking where he was from, where he was going, and how old he was. Moses responded to the man in a friendly way, without answering any of his questions. The man liked to laugh and joke with others on the truck, and he made Moses laugh too.

They stopped at a small settlement where some people got out and more got on. They carried on and stopped again after an hour, and the man with the goats climbed out. Moses helped him lift the goats over the tailgate of the truck and to the ground. "Thanks, child! Go well!" Moses waved at him and the man walked to the side of the road where he was greeted by his friends and children.

When they reached Bangata, the truck stopped for the last time. Everyone was relieved to get out of the bumpy truck and onto firm ground. The passengers departed in different directions, and the truck driver went into a bar. Moses stood by the truck and looked at the road that went up to the school. He remembered when he and Kioso had first set out on their journey. He thought of himself before the journey as one thinks of another person. To Moses, it seemed that if he met that person now, he would not like him. In fact, he would hate him. Then Moses thought of people he did like. People he wanted to be around. He thought of Toroye and the man and woman in the bush. These people did not fight. They were not violent or cruel. They did not shoot people. They did not beat people. They did not look at him like he was an animal. They did not hate him. He thought about it some more: they shared with each other, they gave food, they sheltered people by their fire.

Moses sat on a beer crate outside the bar by the road, thinking of all the people he knew. He thought about the old man with clubfeet. He wondered what happened to him, and if he was still alive and selling oranges. He hoped that he was, that he was the kind of old man who lived forever.

Moses looked up again at the road leading to the school. It was where he was *supposed* to go, but Moses never went where he was supposed to go. Instead he sat in the cold evening air on the crate of empty beer bottles. When the shop closed and the owner took the crate back into his shop, Moses sat on the ground. It grew late and people dispersed, going to their homes and kitchens, children and beds. But Moses felt no cold that night. Eventually he lay down on the ground, just as Toroye would have done, and went to sleep.

The following morning, he rose early and walked onto the road leading east out of town. The big road, the one going far to the ocean and to Dar es Salaam. The road the big trucks drove, travelling between two different worlds—Dar es Salaam and everything else. Moses walked on, the dust from his heels reminding him of when he had walked in the bush with Toroye. He imitated Toroye's walk, which he had come to know well. It made him laugh, walking along in Toroye's choppy gait. When he had had enough walking, he asked for rides from the passing lorries, and eventually one driver stopped for him. He was lucky, because after his long time in the bush, he looked worse than any homeless streetkid. Surprisingly, his sandals had survived the journey, but his clothes were filthy and more stained than ever, and he smelled of a different world, of smoke, fat, livestock, dust. The driver eyed him carefully.

"What are you doing? Walking the highway? Where are you going?"

"Dar es Salaam."

"Dar?" The man—young, with an earring—whistled and laughed. He then opened the door for Moses. And Moses climbed aboard.

"Dar, eh? *Wewe kichaa*, man!" The man shook his head, laughing, put the truck into gear and started down the highway.

Chapter 10

The sun was up now, and the morning had changed from gentle morning, which Moses enjoyed, into angry morning of sun and dust and noise. He sat on a broken slab of concrete with a tangle of iron cables sticking from its side. He watched the road and the people. The hawkers selling newspapers and cigarettes, the people going to work and the people doing nothing, just sitting like he was. *Matatus* passed, horns hooted, people yelled. A fat woman drove by in a small Peugeot. Moses knew she was fat just from the way she sat in the car. Then some birds landed near him and called. Moses looked up into the tree across from him, and saw them sitting on a branch. He watched them and noticed what they did, the way they sang.

It used to be his place, this stretch of road. He was briefly entertained by recognising some faces, shops, and habits. The Indian shop owner stepped out from his store to inspect the chaos of the day, his expression cynical, as if to say, "See what I mean? Just look at these people." He was overweight and his shirt yellowed from days inside the musty shop, smoking black tobacco and chewing betel nut.

After a while, Moses looked over the scene with less interest and rose to leave it.

Back across the open yard and the rail tracks, he passed the glittering broken glass scattered on the ground and the flapping of plastic bags ensnared in the lone acacia tree. The tree stood by itself in the yard, a stubborn reminder of how things might have once looked. Every limb was decorated with plastic bags tangled in its thorns. Moses thought briefly of the piece of plastic bag he had found in the wilderness, and how he had kept it. And the bottle-tops. Here, such things were everywhere. Bottle-tops by the thousands, plastic bags, smouldering piles of burning rubbish, oil stains on the earth where a car had once been repaired. Here he picked up none of it, and walked down further towards the harbour.

At the entrance to the ship hull, he sat. He took off one of his sandals and pried a small goat's-head thorn from the thin rubber sole. He held it between his fingers and looked at it. He wondered where it was from—the huts, the cave, the place he buried Kioso? He flicked it aside. A strong fist-sized beam jutted out from the hull. It was polished smooth from years of hands touching it or using it as a banister to climb down into the hull. Moses put his hand there and rubbed it and looked around. There was nobody home today. The place felt empty. Perhaps the kids were out.

He kicked at a board and then went under it and crawled into his old home. Signs of the living were there: some cigarette butts, a broken bottle, banana peels that were old, but not so old. It was still a good shady place, he thought. He took some old newspaper and swept the boards clean of dust and sand and cigarette butts. He then sat and looked out over the ocean through the cracks in the hull. The blue was brilliant that day, and the sun was strong on the water. He watched a boat pass with two fishermen on board. They looked tired, perhaps returning from a night fishing at sea, one man at the bow looking towards the shore and the other slouched in the back steering them in. The one in front called out to the shore, his arm half bent above his head, his fist clutching the wide tail of a mackerel.

Moses lay down and fell asleep while looking at the sea through the boards. When he woke up, there was only a sliver of light remaining in the day. It was unnerving to wake up in the near dark. He had not intended to sleep all day. He sat upright and looked through the cracks and into the deep blue darkness of twilight. He peered around at his surroundings and the barrenness of it all. He saw the board where Kioso had once etched their names: Heriel, Moses, Kioso . . . He thought of them and how long it had been since he had stayed there with them.

Moses left the hull briefly to find cardboard, matches, and some water to drink. He returned with all three items, as well as a mango. He gathered some rubbish and sticks near the hull and went back inside. He made a small fire and spread the cardboard down for his bed. The fire died quickly, but its small embers glowed nicely and kept him company. He slept again.

The following morning, he set off to look for Mama Tesha. He journeyed through town, stopping for a while at a row of wooden stalls where people were selling medicine—powders in small jars and various barks, roots, branches, and neat bundles of dried leaves tied with strands of sisal. A few women and a man were selling black, tarlike honey from Ugalla, as well as the lighter, cheaper local stuff.

"Moses? My God, is that you?"

"Grace!" Moses ran over to grab her hand, a wide smile over his face. He never knew he would be so happy to see her. And it surprised both of them. He had thought many times of her: her womanliness, her hair and hands that seemed to know how to do things like cook and sew and mend.

"You are so skinny. Where have you been? My God, look at you. Are you okay?"

"Do you still live in that room?" he asked her.

Grace looked down at the wretched boy, filthy, weightless, and gaunt. His eyes were the same, but he looked much older.

"Come with me." She kept his hand in hers as they turned to walk down the street, but then let it go. He was almost as tall as she was, she thought. Not quite, but certainly taller than before. They walked down an alleyway and over to another street, and stopped at a shaded area with tables and chairs and umbrellas. A man was stirring a cauldron of food over a large fire. Some women came and went from inside a small shack where there was another fire for brewing tea and milk for the patrons outside. Grace and Moses sat on the white plastic chairs under an umbrella.

They drank tea and ate plantain and tripe stew. Moses could not finish his food, and Grace pointed at his bowl with her spoon. She still had not smiled.

"What's this? You are not hungry? Look at you. Eat, you boy."

Moses forced more food in his mouth as she wagged her spoon at him again. He had not had such a nice meal in a very long time, but simply could not eat much of it, even though it tasted so wonderful.

"Do you still live in that room?"

Grace sighed and nodded. "Where have you been?" she asked.

It was as if neither wanted to talk about themselves, their lives. For her, it meant discussing the continuation of her life with no improvement. Yes, still in that room, still here. For her, it was a reminder of her stagnation, of dreams unfulfilled, whatever they might have been. A husband maybe, or more money so she could do this or that or move or start again or find work—or anything. And for Moses, where he had been was a long story that he simply wasn't going to tell.

"You know, I remember your room. I remember your bed, exactly how it was. I remember the picture on your wall—you and those people in the country. I remember the cross on the wall. You had pinned it there by itself and it was a bit crooked. I remember your hair and that it was all over the place. I remember that the kanga you were wearing was white and green. Was that your family?"

She looked at him as if wanting to crack a smile at this funny child, but not able to bring herself to do it.

"Yes, it was. You have a good memory."

They ate the rest of the meal without much more talk, both sitting looking at each other, slowly chewing their food.

They finished their food, and she paid and rose to leave.

"Goodbye, Moses. You stay out of trouble, okay? I don't want to find you somewhere."

"Where are you going, Grace? Are you working tonight? Are you going home now?"

"Goodbye, Moses." She paused. "Yes, I am." And she turned and walked off. Moses watched her leave, her wonderful walk, so elegant and neat. He watched her walk the whole way down the road, not stopping once to look in a shop or to turn her head. Just walking, head held straight, off and down the road.

Moses carried on toward Mama Tesha's house, but when he was about halfway there, he stopped and turned back towards the harbour. He did not think why. He just did. Something in him—a physical thing—turned him around.

That night, he saw one of the phantoms roaming the street. He recognised the old man with his glassy white eyes and the web of garbage draped over his shoulders—plastic bags, strips of rags. He remembered how he and Kioso had heckled him once, laughing, saying bad things to the man. The phantom had only waved his arm slowly at them, dismissing all their words in one indifferent sweep. Now Moses looked at him, and he appeared no different—his grey hair in messy curls, with grass and dirt stuck in it. It reminded him of the Ndorobo couple.

The phantom did not look at Moses from the side or make any gesture that acknowledged his existence. Moses continued to watch the man as he approached a rubbish heap steaming with fish parts and foul produce. A pair of wiry cats scattered. The man reached inside the heap, feeling for food, things. He seemed to not notice the violent odour, which Moses could smell from some distance away. He seemed to not even see what he was groping for, but just probed the rubbish, his hands like a heron's bill in muddy water.

The phantom shuffled to within touching distance of Moses, but still did not acknowledge him. Moses rose and walked to the rubbish heap to peer at its contents. He then left the man and walked to the mosque to drink some water from the tap outside. Tomorrow is Friday, he thought, and the Muslim shopkeepers will be handing out coins to beggars.

When he returned to the ship hull, someone was there. A boy like him, but one he did not recognise. The boy lay in the corner, stoned from glue and glossy-eyed like the phantom. Drool came from his mouth and yellow snot from his nose.

"Who are you?" Moses demanded.

The boy did not respond.

"Hey—who are you?" he said again, nudging the boy with his foot.

The boy sniffled and shuffled slightly upright.

"Hey! Say something, you." Moses wanted to kick him. A rage suddenly came over him, and he wanted to slap the boy's face and throw him out onto the beach, into the water. For a moment, he fantasised about drowning him, holding his head under water while he squirmed. Then of holding his face in the sand, in shit, under his shoe, and finally suffocated and dead on the beach for the next day's sun to bake.

The boy only looked up at Moses vacantly. Then he took a sniff of glue from the plastic container he held in his hands.

Moses wanted to scream at him, kick him, beat him. But he didn't. He didn't fulfil his dark fantasies. Instead, he left that place.

For two days, Moses wandered. He walked, drank water at the mosque, and ate very little. He slept in various places. He once returned to the ship hull only to hear strange voices from inside, so he walked away. One night he wandered into a small forest in between some houses and a park. He had always noticed it, but felt it was a dangerous place to go alone because of thieves and men like Prosper, but he wriggled his way into a thicket so dense that only a cat could penetrate it. He smiled at his discovery. Once inside, he was surrounded by thick walls of vegetation. He made a small clearing just large enough for his body and he bedded down like a small antelope, curled, hidden, but with one ear up for danger.

The next day he cut some leafy branches and pulled them into his nest. Every time he came or went, he would make sure that he reinforced the entrance with branches, keeping it hidden and safe. At night he could hear a bushbaby in the trees above. He was sure it was only one, perhaps alone like he was, spending its days curled tight in some tree-crevice and only emerging at the safe hours of

night to find fruits. He could also always hear the barking dogs, which he detested. They carried on like gangs, he thought, so stupidly just one following another.

Toroye would like it here, he thought. He might even be impressed. Moses imagined what it would be like to bump into Toroye walking down the road, and to greet him happily and show him his lair and all the considerations he had made, like the safe entrance and the bed and the place where he could hang things if he had things. There was just enough space to carve out another resting area for Toroye, and he could go cut more branches or find cardboard for him to sleep on.

He thought next of what he would do with Toroye, and where they would go. The harbour? The market? The ship with the new kids? The beach? Grace? But he could not picture Toroye in any of these places, and the thoughts did not make him happy, so he tried to push them from his mind. He lay back and threw the stick he was holding into the canopy of the trees above him. It got tangled in the branches and stayed there, suspended awkwardly, as if about to fall.

When he went to the market the next day, he thought of Prosper only once and briefly. He looked over at the place where Prosper used to hang out, foolish and mean, leaning against the shoeshine stand. Moses looked at it, felt a mixture of anger, time, and faded fear, and then carried

on into the market. The old man with clubfeet was still there. As he approached, he could just make out the stained white hat on his head in the deep shade of his fruit stall. The image was exact and perfect. The same as that time long ago when he ran from this place in terror. Moses walked up.

"From the dead, look at you!" The old man hobbled to his feet, waving and shouting happily.

"My God! Like a skinny dog you are. What is wrong with you? Where have you been? Don't you eat any more? Come sit, boy."

"Hi there, *mzee. Shikamoo*," Moses muttered with a small smile, referring to the man as one does an elder.

"*Marahaba*," the old man replied, impressed by Moses's manners. He then spoke again, this time more softly.

"Really, child, where have you been?"

Moses paused, looked to the side and around.

"I am here," he said at last.

The old man said nothing and offered Moses an orange. They ate, and still the old man said nothing. It was the first time Moses had known him to be silent. The old man then reached low inside some place Moses had never seen, in between the crates and boxes, and pulled out a plastic bag. It was tied up nicely, probably prepared by the man's wife. He carefully untied the knot in the plastic bag. He opened it and placed it on one of the crates. Inside was a meal of fish and rice on a red plastic plate.

"Go fetch some water there, child," he said, motioning to a tap near the market entrance. Moses took a tin jug from the man's side and went to fill it with water. He returned and poured water over the man's hands as he washed them. The man then poured some water for Moses to wash his hands under. Then they ate rice and fish with their hands and did not speak.

The old man wanted to ask many questions of the boy, this child who wandered the streets. So thin, so poor. He thought of his own children, his girl and three boys. His wife at home, who right now would be sweeping the dirt yard outside their shack, clearing out any rubbish that had blown in during the night. What does one do with such a child? A child soon to become a man with nothing but his shirt? And what a shirt it is, held together by strings.

The old man let Moses eat. A few times he began to say something, but stopped. A few times he was about to ask the first of his many questions—what are you going to do now? But he didn't. He sat with Moses and let the boy eat his food. Moses finished the meal, thanked him and rose to leave. The old man took him by the arm:

"So, you'll be here in the morning first thing to help me with those heavy crates, right, my child?"

Moses smiled and perhaps he nodded—the old man could not tell. And in the end, he walked away. And as he walked, he sang Radi in his head, or rather, Radi just seemed to appear there:

The days are too long, so stay with me.
If you are hungry, then I will stay with you.
And if you are lost,
Then I will come to find you.

Author's note: This book was written before the tragic death of André de Kock in Tanzania.